A TASTE OF DIFFERENT DIMENSIONS

15 FANTASY TALES FROM A MASTER STORYTELLER

ALAN DEAN FOSTER

WFP
WORDFIRE PRESS

PRAISE FOR ALAN DEAN FOSTER

"Alan Dean Foster is the modern-day Renaissance writer, as his abilities seem to have no genre boundaries."

—*Bookbrowser*, for *Mocking Program*

"One of the most consistently inventive and fertile writers of science-fiction and fantasy."

—*The Times* (London)

"Alan Dean Foster is a master of creating alien worlds for his protagonists to deal with."

—*SFRevu*, for *Sagramanda*

"Foster's greatest strength remains his world building, easily creating evocative alien landscapes and populating them...."

—*Booklist*, for *Strange Music*

"Amusing ... intriguing ... consistently entertaining."

—*Locus*, for *Lost and Found*

"A winner for all ages."

—*Publishers Weekly*, for *Lost and Found*

"Packed with action, intriguing human and alien characters, and a message of strength through diversity."

—*Library Journal*, for *Drowning World*

CONTENTS

The Taste of Different Dimensions

by Alan Dean Foster

Trade ISBN: 978-1-61475-956-0
eBook ISBN: 978-1-61475-957-7
Hardcover ISBN: 978-1-61475-985-0

Cover design by Janet McDonald
Cover artwork images by Adobe Stock
Kevin J. Anderson, Art Director

Published by
WordFire Press, an imprint of
WordFire, LLC
PO Box 1840
Monument, CO 80132

Kevin J. Anderson & Rebecca Moesta, Publishers

WordFire Press eBook Edition 2019
WordFire Press Trade Paperback Edition 2019
WordFire Press Hardcover Edition 2019
Printed in the USA
Join our WordFire Press Readers Group for free books,
sneak previews, updates on new projects, and other giveaways.
Sign up at wordfirepress.com

❁ Created with Vellum

INTRODUCTION

It is commonly accepted that writing science-fiction is harder than writing fantasy due to the amount of "real world" research that has to go into the former. But as with anything involving art, there are no inviolable rules. Bad science-fiction often features a great deal of poor research. Sometimes none at all. Whereas good fantasy can contain a lot of the same. This is especially true if said fantasy is based on existing lore, folk tales, ethnology, or real-world situations.

The Arabian Nights would be one such example. If you're going to do an Arabian fantasy it's difficult to avoid that seminal collection of tales containing everything from djinn to the adventures of Sinbad the Sailor (a leading SF/Fantasy publisher was called Roc, for example). While a majority of fantasy, including Tolkien, draws upon European folk tale and fantasy tradition, today the avid reader can find fantasies based on everything from Japanese mythology to that of Africa and India. The fact that so many of the great early literature from other countries takes the form of fantasy only tempts writers to make contemporary use of it.

What's difficult to do is to write fantasy that steps outside these obvious precursors. Take China. There are so many stories involving the Monkey King that you could fill a room with Monkey King anthologies. Just as American editors must roll their eyes in exasperation every time another story submission drones on about elves and orcs, wizards with pointy hats and long white beards, and evil sorcerers who have no redeeming social values, so must Chinese editors sputter in frustration at yet the ten thousandth tale featuring some iteration of the Monkey King.

But submit a story, say, where Beijing is stalked at night by a monster given life by that city's notorious pollution, and you might have something. In the story, the municipal authorities might try to trace the monster to the super-sensitive particulate detectors atop the US embassy. Now you have a tale that doesn't rely on thousand-year-old traditional storytelling. *The Global Times* might even buy it.

Or how about a story where an old god submerged by the lake behind the Three Gorges dam threatens to rise up and wreak havoc? Or one where a mermaid (a Chinese mermaid) at Spratley Reef takes offense at the Chinese military chewing up her home? Modern Chinese fantasy can thrive without the Monkey King. Unless some kid suspects the Monkey King is being held in the simian exhibit that's part of a traveling circus motoring about the hinterland.

Similar examples could be given for every country. The point is that fantasy is much more than extrapolation from ancient tradition. More than vampires and werewolves (although I have yet to see a story where a werewolf ends up in a veterinarian's office). If nothing else, humanity has always had a fecund imagination. When sitting around a fire you have to do something besides warm your hands.

Once you have latched onto what you hope is a new idea, or at least a novel variation on an old one, the next step is to maintain the internal logic. Just as if you were writing science-fiction. The difference is that with fantasy you get to make up not just some but all of the rules. But there are still rules. Your djinn can't live in a lamp one minute and a Beverly Hills mansion the next—unless you establish that as one of the rules in your story. Nothing can happen without a reason, no matter how fantastical the scenario. You have to be consistent throughout, even if your story is one about Hieronymus Bosch painting from life.

I hope you find the enclosed tales each a little bit different, but consistent within. Or at least consistently entertaining.

Alan Dean Foster
Prescott, Arizona
June 2018

1 ALI BABETTE

I f you eat regularly at a restaurant, eventually the waiters and waitresses will come to know what you typically order. Especially if it's breakfast or lunch. There used to be such a place here in my hometown called TRISH'S. Some several decades ago, one of the waitresses was a tall, truly beautiful woman. One day when she was taking my regular omelette order I noticed she seemed particularly sad. Inquiring gently, I found out that, unsurprisingly, her dejection involved a guy.

"I've been married three times," she told me. "The first time it was for looks. The second was for money. By the third go-round I wasn't too picky. He turned out to be an alcoholic."

I nodded sagely—as if I knew anything. "So, what are you looking for in a man now?"

She turned thoughtful. "I don't care what he looks like. I don't care if he has any money." She looked down at me. "I just want somebody who will treat me with some decency."

Soda was glad she didn't have to close for the night. Even without being stuck with the responsibility of securing the place, Monday nights sucked. True, a less-than-grand total of four customers since nine o'clock made for no fights, no arguments over who had the next game on the one slightly unsteady pool table, and reasonably clean restrooms, but it also meant next to nothing in the way of tips. When you were young, single, and tending bar in greater New York (actually it was Hoboken, but greater New York sounded so much better), you needed every buck from every jerk. She bid good night to Dave, who would handle the closing, and left.

Only one fool hassled her on the bus on the way home. It was too late and too cold outside even for the average pervert. Glancing left and right before getting off the bus, she assured herself no one was lurking in the shadows waiting to jump her. Concluding the brief reconnaissance, she knew she was luckier than many late-night commuters. Her building was only a block from the bus stop.

It was dark, it was freezing (hey, it was Jersey in January), and she was drained. The weekend had gone pretty good, but now she needed rest. She had the next three days off, and she intended to use every one of them to catch up on her sleep and Those Things What Needed Doing. Maybe Gerry would call. Or Stax. Stax was sharp, looked great, dressed fine, but he was a lazy narcissistic bum. Bit of a raging male chauvinist, too. By contrast, Gerry didn't look like much, but he was pleasant enough and made good money working for the Port Authority and was occasionally nice to her. After five years working steady behind the bar at the DEW DROP INN on Clancy Avenue, and after an equal number of failed relationships, she was ready to sacrifice muscles for money and compliments for kindness. Her mother called it maturing. Soda called it growing tired.

Soon after graduating from Carver High she had discovered that being moderately attractive in the wider world didn't automatically guarantee you the hand of a Prince Charming. It didn't even guarantee you a chance with the Evil Grand Vizer. Most of the guys who wandered in and out of the DEW DROP INN were little more than testosterone-powered lumps of clay.

Not that she was in desperate need of permanent male companionship. By now she was used to being on her own. But—it *would* be nice to have someone warm to curl up next to at night. Someone to confide in, someone you could talk to secure in the knowledge that your words wouldn't be taken the wrong way, wouldn't be twisted into something nasty and hurtful.

She'd had her fill of that.

The pillow caught her eye because of the way it reflected the light that was bolted over the entrance to the apartment building. It caused her to hesitate at the bottom of the landing. A dozen or so heavy cardboard boxes had been dumped beside the stone steps, next to the regular garbage bin. They were pregnant with junk, the refuse of a life or lives too busy to bother with their contents. Most of what she could see in the dim light looked just like that: junk. But the pillow was different.

Nobody was peeking out any of the first-floor windows, watching her. The panes of the old brownstone were dark. No one else in the building that she knew of worked hours as late as she did. Moseying over to the pile of cardboard, she peered closer at the corner of the pillow that protruded from one. The covering material looked like silk, or maybe satin. It did not appear to be stained. Either way, it was a cut above what she had on the second-hand couch in her tiny living room.

After a brief struggle with the box resting on top of it, she pulled it free. It was a throw pillow of average size. Gold tassels decorated the four corners and gold fringe, apparently intact, lined the seam. The fabric itself was silvery. Her couch was a patterned forest green, but the potential contrast didn't concern her. Architectural Digest was unlikely to come calling to do a story on her place any time soon. Intricate embroidery in a script she didn't recognize decorated both sides of the shimmering material. Under her gentle ministrations it fluffed up quite nicely. Finding it almost made up for the lousy night at the bar.

It looked good, snugged in a corner of her couch, resting up against one rolled arm. Setting aside the mug of instant hot cocoa she'd prepared, she reached down to carefully smooth out the fabric so the elegant gold embroidery would show clearly, rubbing her open palm from one corner of the pillow to the other.

On the third pass of her hand, the pillow exploded.

Well, didn't actually explode. Smoke and haze erupted from it, but the only sound was a soft underlying hissing. Afraid that it might contain some harmful substance, she put her hand over her nose and mouth and stumbled backward toward the kitchen. She was hunting for the phone to call 911 when through the rapidly dissipating vapor she found herself staring at a singular figure.

A cat.

Sitting on the couch atop the inexplicably reconstituted pillow, the cat stared back.

This in itself was nothing remarkable. Staring was a common attitude of cats. What *was* extraordinary was the cat's attire. In fact, she mused as she forgot all about the telephone, calling 911, and everything else, *any* cat attire was extraordinary. Cats came clad in fur; long or short. They did not dress in diaphanous silk pantaloons, jewel-encrusted turbans, miniature vests of gold and silver thread, and small boots of crimson silk boasting upturned toes. When they visited apartments in northern New Jersey they tended to arrive via cracked doors or half-open windows, not exploding pillows. Otherwise, the interloper appeared to be a perfectly ordinary gray and black housecat.

That was a very big Otherwise, however.

Clutching her robe tight around her, she swallowed hard. Before she could pause to reflect on the absurdity of it, she found herself asking, "How did you get in here?" Perhaps not surprisingly, the cat rose to stand on its hind legs, crossed its front paws over its chest, and replied, "Thrice you rubbed the enchanted Pillow of Sitting and Sleeping. I came at your command."

"It wasn't a command," she protested, thinking to add, "You can talk."

"Verily, fifty-five languages and one hundred and sixty-two dialects can I speak, plus the languages of the djinn that no human can understand."

"Djinn? You mean, you're a genie?" Aware that she was speaking nasally, she removed her hand from her nose and mouth. If it hadn't hurt the cat, the smoke and mist that had heralded its improbable arrival was probably harmless to her as well. She was tired and bewildered, but otherwise felt all right. Physically, anyway.

"I am the djinn Asami el-Razar el-Babesthi the Magnificent, of the line of Al-Bintetta the Stupendous, of the djinn of fabled Samarkand. The great and ancient Samarkand of trade and legend, not the sorry Central Asian pit stop it is now."

She swallowed. "How—how did you get here?"

"Air courier. I was a gift that was not appreciated, and was peremptorily cast out without the vessel wherein I dwell being appropriately caressed." Burning bright yellow eyes regarded her thoughtfully. "You have released me from the Pillow. Thereby am I commanded by the Great and Almighty Turazin, ruler of all the feline djinn, to grant whosoever caresses my container appropriately, three wishes."

"Three wishes!" This wasn't happening, she told herself. But then, why not? This was Jersey. Anything and everything could happen in North Jersey, and often did. Visions of riches vast enough to embarrass the Lotto began to swim in her head. Or at least, they did until the djinn spoke again.

"Alas, there seems to be a problem."

A catch. There was always a catch. That was true of Jersey, too. "What problem?"

"You are not a cat. I am not a djinn of the human kind. I am a djinn of the Felidae. I am empowered to grant cat wishes to cats. That is one reason why I was not released earlier from the Pillow. The one who dwells high above you and who received me does not associate with cats."

"That's pretty dumb of them. Me, even though I've never been able to afford to keep one, I've always really liked cats. Sometimes I'll feed one or two of the neighborhood strays, but they never stick around."

"Most altruistic of you."

"If you don't mind, I think I'll have to call you Razar. Your full name is a bit of a mouthful for me."

Dropping back down to all fours, the djinn looked around the apartment. "Speaking of mouthfuls, I've been asleep for two hundred and twenty years, and I'm famished. You wouldn't happen to have any cream around, would you? Or a dead mouse?"

"Sorry. Fresh out. Although it shouldn't take long to find rats in this neighborhood. How about some milk?"

Long whiskers and pink nose screwed up disdainfully. "I prefer thick cream. But no djinn can choose its place of release. Milk will do."

She sipped her cocoa and watched the cat as it sat contentedly on her kitchen table and lapped milk from a saucer. "About those three wishes, now. You're sure they have to be cat wishes?"

Sitting back on his haunches, Razar daintily licked his right paw and used it to clean his milk-stained whiskers. "I very much fear that is the way of things. While I cannot conjure mouse or milk for my own meal, I could for example provide my new Master with an unending supply."

"Hey, no way! Remember what I told you about the neighborhood rats. If that's what I wanted, I wouldn't need to wish for it."

Razar the Magnificent belched softly, in most stealthy feline fashion. "Not bad milk. I prefer that what comes from the dromedary, but this was most eminently satisfactory. I confess that beyond my customary bindings I find myself favorably disposed to you—to you—"

"Soda," she replied quickly. "That's not my real name, of course. My real name's Emmaline Ray Coarseguth. From Waco, originally."

"I can see why you prefer the other." The cat turned thoughtful. "As I say, I quite like you, Soda. But the Law is the Law, and I cannot break it. What can I do to favor you within the strictures that are imposed upon me? How about a charmed scratching post that will never wear out?"

"No thanks." She brightened, crossing one leg over the other. Part of her robe fell to one side. "Could you make it, say, an 18th century ivory-

and precious stone-inlaid French marquetry cabinet with a scratchable leg?"

Protruding through small slits in the top of the golden turban, fuzzy ears inclined forward. "Alas, it is not within my power to manifest such transparent circumventions. The wishes I grant must be those any true cat would long for."

This wasn't going as well as she hoped. "How about a lifetime supply of canned tuna?"

Razar brightened and stood up on his hind legs. In that posture he looked terribly cute, she decided, in his admirable miniature genie outfit. "Now that is something I may easily obtain for you! Your first wish?"

"No, no." She waved him off and he dropped back to all fours. "I'm just trying to establish some parameters here, that's all. Actually, I'm not real fond of tuna."

"You have no taste." The cat was clearly disappointed. One paw rose to indicate the rest of the modest apartment. "But your dwelling confirms that."

"Look, I didn't wish for criticism, either. This is nothing that a small bejeweled palace swarming with servants wouldn't fix." She waited a long moment before adding, "I suppose that's out of the question, too?"

Whiskers bobbed as Razar nodded gravely. "No solid gold cat boxes, either. Gold means nothing to a real cat."

Then what would, she pondered? If she was a cat, what would she wish for that would also prove of some value to a human? The djinn had mentioned cat boxes. She doubted wishing for one filled with small diamonds instead of clay litter would fulfill the requirement of asking for something a cat would also want. For that matter, a cat would probably disdain diamonds in its litter box, gemstones being decidedly non-absorptive.

She might be able to wangle a nice bed out of The Magnificent, but she already had a bed. Dammit, this wasn't fair! She had recovered the pillow and freed its torpid occupant. Didn't she deserve a proper reward? So she was taller and had less hair than a Siamese or Calico, so what?

That line of reasoning would gain her nothing but frustration, she realized. It wasn't Razar's fault. He seemed more than willing to please. But it appeared that rules were rules, even for feline djinn. Just like she couldn't serve anyone under 18, and sometimes had to cut off regulars who'd imbibed too much.

No matter how hard she tried, she couldn't think of anything that would appeal to a cat as well as herself. Then it came to her. Setting her empty mug aside, she drew her robe tighter around her. Outside, the cold depth of night still chilled the city.

"Cats love strong smells, right? I want a vial—no, make that a gallon. Yes, that's it. A gallon of the finest perfume."

"*Ashelemak*—so it shall be." Rising again onto his hind legs, Razar brought his front paws together in—well, not a clap. They were cat's paws, after all. It was more like a soft *pouf*. From within the *pouf*, an exquisite oversize decanter appeared, filled to the brim with a bright golden liquid. Delighted, she reached excitedly for the stopper. Removing it, she brought the inner tip toward her nose.

It never got close. Hurriedly, she restoppered the gallon decanter.

"What the hell is *that*? It smells awful!"

"To a human, perhaps." Razar was unapologetic. "To a cat, it is the essence of aromatic beauty."

"But I wanted perfume suitable for a human!" she protested.

Front paws spread wide and the djinn shrugged soft, furry shoulders. "You wished for perfume. I am compelled to bring only that which is intended to satisfy cats, not humans."

She nodded slowly and sat back in the chair. This was going to be harder than she'd imagined. At least the fine crystal decanter was salvageable—provided she could ever get that hideous smell out of it. And she'd wasted her first wish. She wouldn't make that mistake again. She couldn't afford to. Perhaps she should try to be as realistic as possible about the situation, scale back her wants.

"What about a lifetime credit at the Fulton Fish Market?" Visions of endless lobster dinners sallied through her head.

"Your second wish?"

She shrugged. She was dead tired, and the conundrum she faced seemed insurmountable. "Hey, why not?"

"*Arelemoku!*" Paws traced a complex pattern in the air. By now she was used to the smoke and vapor. It seemed unnecessarily theatrical.

A square piece of parchment appeared on the water-stained coffee table in front of her. Frowning, she leaned forward to get a better look at it. "This isn't a card granting credit."

"Of course not." Razar shook his head slowly. "Did you think a cat would carry a credit card, or any kind of human document?" One paw tapped the parchment. "You must memorize this. As soon as you have done so, it will vanish."

7

"What is it?" she asked dubiously.

"A detailed map of the market to which you wish unrestricted entrance, showing every entryway and exit plus the times of day and night when they are never watched. During those times, you may slip freely into each booth and secure whatever seafood you desire. This ability will now be with you forever."

"I can't steal fish! That isn't what I wanted. Even if I could do it, I can't spend that kind of time away from work."

Razar the Magnificent shrugged again. "A cat could. Any cat would be thrilled to be granted this kind of access."

Two wishes gone. She absolutely, positively, could not waste the third and last. "You said that you liked me. But you're not being very helpful."

"I'm sorry. Truly I am." He sounded sincere. "Don't you see, Soda? The enormity of the problem facing you has defeated many, many humans down through the ages." He sighed. "It is ever the same when I am accidentally called forth by a human instead of by a cat. Humans and cats simply want different things. There is no way around it." He met her eyes evenly. "You might as well spare yourself the mental agony and just wish for something simple to get this over with. A toy play mouse, perhaps, or a ball of string. And could I have some more of that milk, please?"

While she poured him another saucerful, she ruminated on the unfairness of it all. A real genie, three genuine wishes—and all three of them apparently useless to her. She could think of many things to wish for: all of them priceless to a cat and far less so to a human.

She could wish for a lifetime of good health, and probably receive it—provided she was willing to see veterinarians for the rest of her life. She could ask to never go hungry again, and probably wouldn't—provided she was willing to eat cat food. Face it: cats' wants were simple and straightforward. It seemed they did not, did not ever, coincide with those of human beings.

Except perhaps ...

She straightened in the kitchen chair. It was hard and cold against her back. Like so many of the things in her life. "Here is my third wish, Razar."

He stopped lapping and rose one more time onto his hind legs. "Are you certain, Soda? I truly feel for you. But believe me when I say that you have been preceded in your frustrations. I hope that I may grant you something a little useful, at least, before I must leave you."

Having given the matter considerable thought and come to a resolution, she nudged the saucer closer to him. This time, she was reasonably certain what she was going to ask for would be understood by any cat. Or at least, by any female cat. "My third wish is for a male companion for the rest of my life. One who is forever kind, thoughtful, and considerate. One who won't abuse me, or curse me, or steal my paycheck. One who won't spend all his time watching television, or complaining about my cooking, or the way I look when I wake up in the morning. One who'll sleep beside me in bed, and help to keep me warm, and whose love will be undying, no matter where I live or if I put on a little weight when I grow old."

The djinn nodded understandingly, impressed by her wisdom. Reaching toward the ceiling with both paws, he hissed the command *"Asenarelt!"*

There was a sizable *pouf* of mist. When it cleared, he was still there. Only now his fine raiment had gone, turban and slippers and vest and pantaloons and all, down to the last gleaming jewel. Only he remained. Reaching out as he contentedly resumed sipping his milk, Soda slowly stroked the head and back and tail of Razar the Magnificent, late of glorious and splendid ancient Samarkand. Glancing up from the milk, he winked at her. Then he began to purr.

She was entirely content.

2 THE WHITE HOTEL

*S*ometimes *you wonder what a particular dream might be like. Or even if it is a dream. The whole "the waking world is really a dream," as typified by films like* The Matrix, *is a bit of an overdone trope now. That doesn't mean you can't imagine what one would be like. Or if a dream of your own might carry some weight with someone else.*

They say dreaming is useful. That it helps to clear old detritus out of memory. Could dreaming be useful in other ways? Hard to say. What is certain is that dreams, a la Lovecraft, can sometimes provide the basis for stories.

Not that this tale is a dream of mine. One of the perks of writing fantasy is that you get to dream all the time. That's the easy part. Writing it down is what takes time, and a bit of discipline....

The room was beautiful. King-size bed, Empire-style lamps on end tables, thick pile rug, heavy blackout curtains, wall TV, and everything executed in a rich, creamy white with brilliant gold trim. Even the wet bar, except for the cut crystal glasses, was all burnished gold and glossy ivory.

Turning a slow circle, Edda took it all in. It made no sense. What was she doing in such a place? She certainly couldn't afford it, not on her income. Had someone tipped her with a gift certificate for a weekend at some fancy uptown establishment? She couldn't remember.

High-falutin' fancy or not, the TV only played expensive pay-per-view movies. She couldn't get any other channels, not even network. She ought to call the management and complain, but for some reason she didn't feel like it. Instead, she wandered into the bathroom.

If anything, it was even more impressive than the sleeping area. The designer had done their work well. She took in the glistening white sunken marble bathtub with its gold fixtures. Naturally, the little bottles of shampoo and conditioner and body oil matched the rest of the décor. She smiled to herself as she slipped out of her clothes and ran the bath. If the color scheme was consistent throughout, this was one hotel that wouldn't have any difficulty finding soap to match its bathrooms.

All rising steam and tickly foam and warm liquid caresses, the bath felt wonderful. Afterwards, she dried herself with one of the plush, unmonogrammed towels and tried a touch of the complimentary body perfume. It seemed almost sinful to climb back into her plain, everyday attire, but except for the complimentary bathrobe hers were the only clothes in the room. Perhaps she'd left a suitcase down by check-in, waiting to be brought up. She tried to call the bell desk, but like the TV, the phone didn't work.

Idiot, she admonished herself. If the phone's out of order, you can't very well use the phone to notify the hotel that the phone is broken. She'd have to tell someone in person. Feeling wonderfully refreshed from her bath, she checked her hair in the bedroom mirror, opened the white door, and stepped out into the hall.

It was as white as her room. Pure, untrammeled white, from the soft carpet underfoot to the snowflake pattern on the wallpaper. White except for the gold trim on the door jambs and wainscoting, the room numbers themselves, and the elegant but simple light fixtures that flooded the corridor with gentle white light. She made a note of her room number: 9432. As she headed down the hall she marveled at the ability of the unseen hotel staff to keep so much whiteness so astonishingly dirt and stain free in the face of what must be a steady flow of guests.

Turning a corner, she found herself facing another corridor. With a mental shrug, she started down it. Must be one of the bigger chains, she thought as she padded along, because this was certainly one of the bigger hotels she had ever been inside. Not that she had stayed at many hotels. Motel 6 lay at the upper end of her travel budget. Reaching the end of the hall, she turned another corner. Found herself facing another corridor.

She was getting frustrated. If she could just find a house phone, she'd call in the message about her broken phone. But there was no house phone. No house phone, and no bank of waiting elevators, white or otherwise. She turned another corner.

Another corridor. And another after that. And another.

She started running. Her mounting panic was multiplied by the fact that ever since she'd left her room she'd encountered no one else, not a single solitary perambulating soul. Not a guest, not a maid, not a bellman. Having apparently forgotten to bring her own phone and not owning a watch, she didn't know what time it was. Come to think of it, she didn't remember seeing a clock in the room. That seemed a peculiar oversight for so well furnished a hotel.

Where was everybody? Even if it was, say, ten in the morning, and the hotel's business clientele had gone off to work, staff should be present; stripping beds, restocking minibars, changing linen. But there was no one. No one, and no noise. She heard no conversation passing, no vacuum cleaners humming, no televisions whispering through closed doors.

Until she heard, off in the distance, a faint howling.

It should have frightened her. No—it should have terrified her, left her trembling in her stylish but eminently practical shoes. The sound wasn't pleasant, and it certainly didn't make her feel any better, but she dealt with it stolidly, as she had all the other disappointments in her young life.

There it was again. Closer? She couldn't tell. Had someone left their dog running loose in the hallways? *Where was everybody?*

She began retracing her steps. It wasn't easy, because some of the corridors branched. As she ran back in the opposite direction, she kept an eye out for the elevators, in case she had somehow missed them. There had to be elevators. Her room number being 9432, she reasoned, she had to be on the ninth floor of the hotel.

The howling was definitely closer now. Or was it more of a growl? She couldn't be sure, and she didn't think she wanted to stop and find out. Though she was in good physical condition, she had been running for a while, and her lungs were starting to labor. Breathing hard, she turned a corner. And another. Another.

9432. She reached for the handle. Impossible to tell how near, or how far, lay the source of the howling. It seemed to drift in and out of her hearing. It struck her forcefully then that she had no key. A deliberate and increasingly frantic search of the pockets in her blouse produced nothing. The corridor stretched away to left and right; white, empty, echoing. Taking a chance, she reached out and tried the handle.

To her immense relief, the door opened easily.

It also closed tightly behind her. A quick glance was enough to show that she was indeed back in her room. The empty bottles in the bathroom, the used towels, were proof enough of that. She could no longer hear the howling, growling. The dog, or whatever, that had been making the noise had gone elsewhere. A determined expression set on her pale but not unattractive face, she walked over to an end table and tried the phone again. Still broken; not even a dial tone. What now?

Walking over to one of the two windows, she found the center and pulled the heavy curtains apart. Expecting to confront the city, to see some other tall building opposite the hotel, she found her vision flooded with whiteness. A whiteness that could not come from a heavy snowfall, since it was September. A whiteness that overwhelmed everything else. That was when it hit her. That's when it all made sense.

She woke up in her own bedroom. It was far less fancy than the hotel room she had dreamed, but at least everything in it worked: the phone, the TV, the clock radio whose red numerals ticked over silently as she eyed it. Three forty-six in the morning. A little early. The alarm wouldn't turn on KXLW for another forty-five minutes yet. Plenty of time to get to Karoly's Restaurant and be ready for the breakfast shift. That's where she worked; Karoly's. Breakfast through lunch shift. She liked the schedule. It gave her time in the afternoon to do the ordinary things nine-to-five workers had to rush to accomplish, from going to the bank to marketing, without having to hurry or fight commuter traffic or worry about the creeps who stalked the city streets after dark.

It wasn't such a bad dream, she mused as she dressed. She'd had far more upsetting ones. The unseen howling thing hadn't been very nice, but neither had it been a vision of devouring teeth and bulging eyes and bloody fangs. It had been just another dream. Another dream, another day. One step closer to the new TV she'd been eying in the window of the JR Electronics shop on Second Avenue.

Work passed uneventfully, as always. Evening brought a trip to the movies with Darlene, her best friend. Coffee and cake afterwards, then home. Time enough to watch the early news, and then sleep.

She was back in her room in the white hotel. 9432. Same layout, same furnishings, only the linens had been dutifully changed and the bathroom restocked.

By the fourth night she knew it was a dream when she was in it. Stuck with it until it went away or changed, she decided to relax and enjoy the experience; the luxurious bath, the classy radio that played odd but enjoyable stations, the television that played only pay movies (hey, she wasn't being billed, so why not indulge?). The lack of a view didn't bother her. In Manhattan, that would just translate to another building across the street anyway. On several occasions, she left the room to take walks down the corridors. Every time, she saw no one else. Twice, she heard the howling and returned quickly to her room. Twice, there was nothing, no noises, leaving her free to explore. But she never found the elevators, or saw another living thing. Or another dreamed thing, she would remind herself.

The dreams didn't affect her sleep, or her work. She was not the type to struggle against such things. But by the second week of having the same dream over and over, she found herself beginning to get a little bored. By the third, she began to wonder if perhaps it wouldn't hurt to see a psychologist. She told Darlene about the dreams, but her friend and fellow waitress had no suggestions to offer beyond recommending that Edda try a good, strong, over-the-counter sleeping pill. After hesitating, she did just that. It didn't make any difference. At some indeterminate time after falling asleep, she inevitably found herself back in the white hotel, room 9432.

It was at the end of the third week that she encountered, quite unexpectedly and upsettingly, the source of the growling.

She was jogging around the corner past room 9647 when she came up short. The howling growling was louder than usual, though not disturbingly so. But for the first time in the dream, she was not alone. There was a figure, another person, at the far end of the hallway. She knew he was the source of the sound because he growled at her when their eyes met. He was immense: six eight or nine, and massive—maybe four hundred pounds. He had to bend slightly to clear the ceiling. His face was red, florid, clean-shaven, and he had blue eyes and short brown hair. He was wearing scuffed work jeans, hiking boots, and a red plaid flannel shirt. The outfit should have placed him somewhere in upstate Maine, not Manhattan. He looked surprised.

"What are you doing here?" he boomed. His voice was deep and threatening.

Here? What did he mean, "here"? This was a dream, the dream of the white hotel. Nothing more.

"Get out!" he roared. "You don't belong here! Get out, *now!*" He started in her direction. With each step he took toward her, his weight made the floor shiver under her feet.

Dream or no dream, she turned and ran. She was faster than him, but that enormous stride kept him close. All the while, he kept bellowing accusingly at her. She didn't pause to reply. Her only interest in life right now, or in dream, was to find the safety of room 9432.

She sensed him closing on her as she turned what she hoped was the last bend. Then she was fumbling for the door handle. A glance up the corridor showed him barreling around the corner, moving so fast that he slid slightly and slammed into the opposite wall, cracking the perfect pale plaster. His huge hands, calloused and big as meathooks, were outstretched toward her and his face was full of blind pain.

The door opened. Inside, she slammed it shut, flipped the lock, and retreated toward the bed. Something heavy hit the door hard. It shook, but held. On the other side, moaning fury had replaced words and growls. The pounding and the howling continued for a while longer. Then they went away, not abruptly as if the huge figure had suddenly gone silent, but fading into the distance.

Chest heaving, she approached the door cautiously. A glance through the peephole showed nothing on the other side. Still, she hesitated. It was still only a dream, she told herself firmly. And nothing in a dream can hurt you, right? She pushed down on the lever and opened the door.

The corridor was silent as after a new-fallen snow. There was no sign of the man who had pursued her. She closed the door. Retreating back into the room, she turned on the radio and drew herself the hottest bath she could stand.

The next day, she saw a registered psychologist. She saw him several times, despite the strain it put on her budget. Her other dream, the one that had the new TV in her apartment, receded a little further into the future. The psychologist was very nice, and very earnest, and utterly useless. And of course, nothing he said or suggested stopped the dreams.

For a while she dreaded going to bed and falling asleep. As for the dreams, sometimes the giant figure materialized to chase her, other times he was absent. On the night of the Wednesday of the fourth week, as he was chasing her with outstretched hands and screaming at her to get out, to go away, that she didn't belong, a thought struck her that did not come from the well-meaning psychologist, or from Darlene, or even from Oprah.

Maybe, just maybe, this wasn't *her* dream. It was a crazy idea, but no crazier than what was happening to her. Maybe that was why the figure was always telling her to get out, that she didn't belong. Maybe it was somebody else's dream. Maybe it was *his* dream. Perhaps that was why he was so angry, and so insistent that she leave, that she didn't belong.

Could you be in someone else's dream? Certainly you could appear in it. Friends and family had often appeared in her other, normal, ordinary dreams. If other people could appear in her dreams, then certainly she could appear in someone else's dream. What was abnormal was her realization that that might be the case. But she didn't know the big man. She had never met him, had never even seen him from a distance. She was positive of that. You wouldn't forget someone of his dimensions. Of course, that didn't mean that *he* had never seen *her.*

What if it wasn't an accurate representation? she told herself. Not everyone always appeared as themselves in dreams. It went a long way toward explaining the white hotel. She felt sure that if given the choice (as much choice as one had in dreams), that if it was her dream, she would have dreamed up a nice, colorful South Seas island beach resort. The white hotel was the big man's dream, not hers.

Such thoughts occupied her all that next day at work, so much so that she actually forgot that Mr. Mackleroy always took whole wheat toast with his omelet and not white. A regular, he was more surprised than upset, and they shared a friendly chuckle over it. He tipped her the same as usual.

That night, she did all the usual things she did before retiring. Could a resolve made while awake hold true even in sleep? She hoped to find out.

For a while, she was afraid it would be one of those dreams that found her entirely alone in the white hotel. Then, outside room 9311, she heard the first howling. Advancing deliberately toward it, she waited until it grew loud enough for her to be sure. Then he was there, at the far end of the hallway as always. And as always, seeing her, he raised his huge hands and started toward her, shouting for her to leave, to go away.

Turning, she fled at a steady pace. There was no panic in her now, since she knew from experience exactly how fast he could run. She kept the distance between them constant as she turned corner after corner. Then the door to her room lay just ahead. She'd left it open. But this time, instead of entering, she whirled to face the oncoming hulk. Hands on hips, lips set firmly, she adopted the same attitude she used when unruly college students tried to confuse her with their orders or pick her up for a casual Saturday night date. The product of six years spent dealing with the breakfast shift in Manhattan, the pose always worked.

But as those glaring eyes and thick fingers came steadily nearer, she found herself trembling a little inside, and wondering if she might not be doing something really, really stupid.

"I'm not going anywhere!" she heard herself shouting. Her voice echoed off the snowflake wallpaper, the gold-trimmed wainscoting, and the gold-metal light fixtures. "This is *your* damn dream! You think I *want* to be here? I like to dream of waving coconut palms and well-tanned beach boys, not some damn deserted hotel, no matter how nice it is!"

The figure drew nearer, nearer—and slowed. The big man stopped, those massive grasping hands falling slowly to his sides. "You don't belong," he insisted. But this time he declaimed in a mumble, and not a shout.

"I know that." She lowered her own voice. "Believe me, I couldn't agree with you more. But here I am, until I wake up, and there isn't a damn thing I can do about it."

He gazed down at her out of eyes that were suddenly sad instead of angry. "Wake up?"

Her lips parted slightly. Not only was she in his dream, if his words were to be believed it appeared that he didn't know this *was* a dream. Crazier and crazier, said Alice. She proceeded to explain things to him.

He sat down in the hall, his wide backside dimpling the carpet, leaning his massive bulk up against one wall. In all that whiteness and gold, their clothing provided the only other color. She told him everything: how she had begun to revisit this same dream every night, how she had come to the conclusion that it wasn't her dream and that it therefore had to be his. She told him everything she had discovered about the white hotel, from the excellent bathroom accoutrements that were provided afresh every night to the dysfunctional telephone and the television that only played pay movies.

He listened to it all carefully, in silence. Without howling or growling or threatening. Then he rose and tentatively extended a hand. "Want— would you like to see my room?"

She hesitated, newly uneasy. It was an invitation to a kind of intimacy she wasn't sure she wanted to share. But she wasn't waking up yet, and it was something new and different, and despite his size he no longer seemed quite so threatening. So she accepted, warily, and walked with him, not taking his hand in case his attitude changed suddenly and she had to make a run for it.

After the usual twists and turns, they halted outside a room. On the door was the number 9665. It looked like any other hotel room door. It looked like her own. He pushed down on the handle, and entered.

The place was a mess. The television had been ripped off the wall and lay on the floor, smashed. The phone handset had been stomped to pieces. Linens lay scattered about, as if the bed hadn't been made in weeks. The bathroom was filthy; the tub sporting a thick dark ring, the sink full of soap scum, the empty bottles of shampoo and conditioner and body lotion lying in a heap. The shower curtain hung limp, half the rings having been pulled out. An unpleasant smell hovered in the vicinity of the toilet.

"I'm sorry," he told her. "It always ends up like this. I can't seem to help myself. I guess—I guess I get angry, and go a little crazy. And then ..."

"And then you run screaming through the halls," she finished for him. Dream or no, she knew she ought to have been afraid. But she wasn't. There was about the room an aura of desperation, not homicidal madness.

He nodded. "For a long time, it was always by myself. Then I started to see you, and that made me angry, too. I'm not sure why, but it did. I guess because you didn't belong. Because you hadn't been invited." He indicated the disarray. "Does your room look like this?"

She shook her head, and had to smile. "I guess I'm a little neater than you, even in dreams."

He looked away. "Are you going to wake up now?"

"Not yet." On impulse, she reached out and took his hand. "Let's take a walk, first. I want to try something. I've wanted to try it for a while, but I kept running into you, and I never could finish." She started for the door.

He resisted. "I—can't."

She looked back up at him. "Why not? What do you mean, you can't? It's your dream, isn't it?"

"I don't know that. I don't know what this is. I only know what you've told me."

She pondered a moment. "All right then," she said finally. "I'm telling you to come with me." She tugged again, firmly. If he didn't want to come with her, she knew, there was no way she could force him. It would have been like trying to drag a mountain.

He took a step. "If you say it's okay ..." He was still unsure.

"What have you got to lose?" She flashed him her best smile, the one that often resulted in double tips. "It's only a dream."

They left the door to his room open, the shambles showing clearly behind them. It wasn't as if it was going to upset the maid, she knew. Purposefully, she led him down corridor after corridor, turning one corner after another. She'd never managed to get past 9876 in one direction or 9202 in the other because she'd always been confronted by her new companion, and had been forced to turn and retreat back to her room. Now, with him in tow, there was nothing to stop her from continuing onward.

She hoped.

They passed 9877. Then 9910. And 9925, 9951, 9978. And finally, 9998 and 9999, both of which boasted double doors and were obviously the entrances to exclusive suites. As always, no noise came from behind the tightly closed portals. But ahead lay something singular, something previously unencountered.

The end. The end of a corridor. It was demarcated by another door. The door was marked like all the others, but was also unlike them. It did not have a number.

On the door she read the words FIRE EXIT.

"Come on," she told him. The great weight of him held back.

"No," he murmured. There was dread in his voice. "I—I can't."

"Sure you can." She looked back up at him. No fury in him now, no howling. Only fear. "It's your dream, whether you believe it or not." She let go of his hand. "I'm trying it even if you won't."

He didn't move; just stared apprehensively down at her. Reaching out, she pushed against the door. It moved. Shoving it all the way open, she found herself looking at a wide, open, windowless stairwell. Like everything else in the white hotel, it was devoid of color. It looked a little dingy, a little less perfect than the hallways and her room, but that was only to be expected of an emergency exit. Ninth floor, she thought. They had a modest descent ahead of them.

"Come on," she urged him again. When still he hesitated, she put her hands on her hips once more in that well-practiced no-nonsense waitress pose and cocked her head sideways at him. "You really in a hurry to go back to that filthy room?"

It required a visible effort for him to take a step forward—but he did. "No," he told her firmly. "No, I'm not."

The stairs led down. At the first landing, the presumed eighth floor, she tried the door. It was secured, as fire exit stairwell doors often are. That meant the door directly above them that led back to the ninth floor would now also be locked. What if all the access doors were secured like this? What if they couldn't get back to their respective rooms, and found themselves trapped in this empty, cold, silent stairwell? It didn't matter, she told herself. Eventually, they would wake up, exiting their respective hotel rooms or this stairwell. There was no danger. She kept telling herself that as they continued to descend.

Eventually the stairwell bottomed out, terminating on a slab of dirty, whitened concrete. If the white hotel held true to hotel form, this should be the escape door, the one leading to the street outside, or to an underground garage, or to the hotel lobby. If it was locked—if it was locked then all they had done was make a useless descent from the floors above.

"What now?" The voice from behind her sounded apprehensive.

She gave a little shrug. "We go out," she told him. Putting her right hand on the heavy fire door, she pushed, leaning her weight into it.

To the nurse's credit, she managed to muffle her scream of surprise. Taking a stunned step backward, she bumped into the IV rack. Transparent bags full of costly liquids jangled but did not fall from their supportive hooks. Plastic tubing rattled but did not disconnect.

The boy in the bed was twelve. Opening his eyes, he blinked once at the ceiling before looking over at the shaken white-clad woman standing by the side of his bed. He peered down at the tubes that ran into him; into his arms and into his side. The needles that penetrated his skin itched. Then he looked up at the nurse again. For a grown-up, she was acting awfully weird.

"Can you call my mom? I don't feel so good." He licked his lips as best he could. "And could I have something to drink, please? I'm awful thirsty."

It was three o'clock in the morning, but the floor supervisor at the 3A nursing station didn't hesitate. She called the doctor at home and woke him.

Edda opened her eyes. Time to make the coffee, do her face, and get dressed. It was Monday, and Karoly's was always busy on Monday. She stretched, preparatory to rising.

Pain shot through her.

What the hell? she thought. She started to get up. More pain, holding her down. What on Earth was going on? She'd been dreaming—she knew that much. The white hotel again, as usual. Last night's dream had been different somehow, but in the haze of first light she couldn't remember the details. The more awake she became, the farther they receded from memory. They didn't matter anyhow. What did matter was the pain.

Maybe she'd gone to sleep in an awkward position. Struggling against the hurting, she made herself sit up. That's when she saw that something —no, not something: everything—was wrong.

Her room was different. In its place was a smaller bed, with a six-sided metal bar running vertically above it. A handle hung from the bar. There were also horizontal metal bars on either side. Where her drawer and mirror combination should have been was a window and a single chair. The color scheme was all wrong as well, as was the lighting. Nothing was as it should be. The TV was there, but it was the wrong model, and in the wrong place.

A figure was sitting in a second chair, off to her left. She frowned momentarily before she recognized it. "Darlene? What are you doing here?"

The figure straightened, coming out of its own slumber. Then the eyes of her best friend widened and her mouth opened in an *O* of surprise.

"*Edda?* Oh my god, Edda!" Rising from the chair, Darlene rushed the bed. Reaching over the metal bars, she threw her arms around her friend. She was crying—no, she was bawling like a baby.

"Hey, take it easy." More than a little bewildered, Edda let her own arms slip uncertainly around her friend's back, patting gently. "It's okay. What's wrong?" She let her eyes roam again, let them identify and analyze her surroundings. She began to comprehend. At first none of it made any sense, and then gradually, it did. "I'm in a hospital, aren't I?"

Still crying, Darlene stepped back. Wiping at her eyes, unable to stop from sobbing, she fumbled for a button attached to the side of her friend's bed, finally managing to depress it. A nurse arrived. The nurse took one look at the woman in the bed and disappeared back the way she had come, reappearing moments later with another nurse and a doctor. They fussed over the patient until Edda couldn't stand it any longer.

"I'm okay, people, I'm okay. Give me some room, for cryin' out loud!"

Red-eyed, Darlene moved to stand next to the attending physician. "Is she—she's going to be all right now, isn't she?"

The doctor's beard was mostly gray, his manner that of a man who had just dumped a dollar into the progressive slot at a local casino only to see five sevens line up.

"Yes, I—yes, she's going to be all right. This is amazing, just amazing. Wonderful, but amazing." He leaned forward slightly and smiled. "You don't try to go anywhere, young lady. You just relax, until I can get back. I won't be long." Turning, he hurried out the door. It was the first time Darlene had ever seen a doctor in a hospital *hurry* from a patient's room.

Pulling her chair close, she sat back down next to the bed and reached out to rest her hand on her friend's arm. "A lot of people have been real worried about you, you know? Me, the staff at Karoly's, your regulars. A lot of people love you, Edda."

"What happened?" the woman in the bed wanted to know. "I remember getting home from work yesterday and going to bed. And dreaming. Like I've been dreaming for weeks now. About the white hotel. Only, last night was different, somehow."

"White hotel? Getting home from work yesterday?" Darlene's tone as well as her expression reflected utter bewilderment. "Hon, you've been in this bed for almost a month. In a coma." She sat straighter in the chair. "You don't remember any of it, do you? You were leaving Karoly's. Must have had something on your mind. Guy was speeding, trying to pass the taxis, trying to beat the light. You stepped out and he hit you. Knocking you thirty feet, I'm told. They say you hit the street and bounced like a rag doll. You've been in here ever since."

Edda gaped over at her friend, trying to make sense of insensible words. She still hurt, but the longer she sat up, the more the pain continued to recede. "C'mon, Darlene. I was at work *yesterday*. I've been going to work every day until today. I remember everything. Waiting on customers. Screwing up Mr. Mackleroy's toast. The five-dollar tip I got last Friday. And the dreams. I remember dreaming every night, for weeks. About the white hotel. I remember talking to you about it, seeing a psychologist, trying sleeping pills. I remember shopping, going to the movies with you, cutting my leg while shaving one night." Her voice fell slightly. "I remember everything."

Her friend just stared at her. Stared for a long moment that stretched into several. Then she rose and walked over to the computer monitor that was mounted on the wall. Beneath the computer, on an attached shelf, was a folder. Though she really wasn't supposed to, she picked up the folder and brought it back to the bed, handing it to Edda with a nod.

"Read it for yourself. Almost a month you've been here."

Edda looked at her friend, glanced down at the folder, then back up at her friend. She opened the folder. She read.

"They were afraid you weren't going to come out of it," Darlene was saying. "You were banged up pretty bad. Your head—you hit your head real hard." She summoned up a smile that was full of warmth and relief. "I was afraid I was never going to be able to talk to you again. And now ..." The tears threatened to flow again. "You just—woke up."

Edda continued to read. The words, the black print, the hand-written notations in typical barely legible doctor's scrawl, could not be denied. "But—everything else. Everything I just told you. It was all—it was so real, Darlene."

Her friend had to laugh. The sound seemed to lighten the room. "As many drugs as they had you on, I'm not surprised, girl! Don't you get it? You were dreaming...."

In spite of, or perhaps because of, their astonishment, they discharged her the next day. They made her promise to come back. For a follow-up, and to answer some questions. After all, she had made history of a sort, and they could hardly be blamed for wanting to document it.

As they wheeled her out (she could have walked, but—regulations) with a beaming Darlene at her side, she happened to note the number of her room: 9432. A sudden small, indefinable thrill ran through her.

"Stop!"

Startled, the nurse complied without thinking. "What is it, miss? Are you okay? Is something wrong?"

"No, nothing's wrong. I'm fine. I'd just like to—I'd like to go another way, if we can?"

Darlene looked at her funny, but she was insistent. The nurse had no objection. She'd learned to deal with all kinds of last-minute requests. "Which way then, miss? Do you know the corridors? You were unconscious when they brought you up from surgery."

"I want ..." She hesitated. How could she say it without it sounding outlandish? So she just said it anyway. "I want to go by room 9665."

The nurse exchanged a glance with Darlene, who looked blank. Turning the wheelchair, they retraced their steps, heading for a different bank of elevators.

Room 9665 was empty, the bed recently remade with fresh linens, the chairs unoccupied, awaiting a patient. Edda gazed into it until she could sense her companions growing uneasy.

"Okay. We can go."

The nurse realigned the chair and resumed pushing. In the elevator on the way down, Edda thought to ask, "Do you know who the last person in that room was?"

The questions discharging patients ask, the nurse thought to herself. "Little boy. Robert Lukens. He was suffering from something serious, I know that. I don't remember exactly what it was. His room wasn't on my rounds. Some kind of serious cancer, I think. Somebody said something about it suddenly going into spontaneous remission. His parents came down yesterday from somewhere up north and took him home." She smiled at the remembrance. "That sort of thing doesn't happen too often in here, and it's always nice to hear stories like that. Just like yours, Miss Lorelheim."

Edda nodded but said nothing. The elevator doors opened and she was wheeled out into the lobby. People were everywhere. She saw Darlene's little compact parked out front, in the pick-up zone. It was an intense white: the whitest white she was sure she'd ever seen.

3 TWO-CENTS WORTH

I *n the Spring of 2003 I and an Indian driver soon-to-be-friend spent a month driving 2,000 miles across northern India. New Delhi to Agra, then west all around Rajasthan, the Thar Desert north to Jaipur, Udaipur, Pushkar, Ranthambore, and eastward via Orchha, Kahjuraho, Jabalpur, the Kanha of Rudyard Kipling's Jungle Book, and down to Nagpur. From there, following a two-hour interrogation in a tiny office by a local airport Customs officer who was certain I was a drug courier, I flew to Kolkata and onward to Darjeeling. In that mountain town the eponymous tea is great but the view across the valley of Kanchenjunga, the third-highest mountain in the world, with Everest in the far distance, is more memorable still.*

Likewise memorable was a brief encounter my driver and I had at an outdoor snack bar on the road between Khajuraho and Jabalpur. It has stayed with me ever since. Not haunted me, but stayed with me.

Which is not to say it couldn't haunt someone else....

It was April, and the heat was unrelenting. By May and certainly by June it would become unbearable, and people would begin to die. Knowles knew that the misery would persist until the monsoon arrived sometime in late June or early July. Not that it mattered to him. In a day or two he would be on a plane back to London, his business in Agra complete. Everything was going swimmingly and he foresaw no roadblocks to closing the deal. The contract had been hard-won, of course. Any time you did business with Indians, it always was. That made the terms he had been able to extract all the more satisfying. One rose, he firmly believed, to the level of one's competition.

This morning's difficult, occasionally fractious discussion had left his throat drier than he had realized. Uncharacteristically, he had neglected to leave the meeting with a bottle of something cold and refreshing. Outside the steel and air-conditioned cocoon of his Mercedes, the great living sea that was Mother India heaved and surged and rumbled around him. Camels and the great wooden disks that were the wheels of the single-axle carts they pulled slowed but did not stop traffic. Neatly dressed men, women, and sometimes children on buzzing motorbikes and scooters skittered in and out of the mass of traffic like angry waterbugs navigating a crowded swamp. Three-wheeled powered rickshaws, mostly painted green and yellow, *pocketa-pocketaed* along on the sidelines, trying to get their passengers or cargo to their respective destinations while keeping out of everyone else's way. Astoundingly overloaded Tata and Ashok-Leyland trucks, not one of which would meet minimum safety standards in Europe or America, lumbered through the mass of traffic with saurupodian grace while engaged in a gruff, eternal ballet with ancient, wheezing, rusty buses not one of which could boast of glass in a single window.

Their weight distributed with Euclidian precision, a family of five balanced on a single motor scooter squeezed past on his right: father, mother, and three small kids. It was not a circus act; just classic Indian commuting. Idly, Knowles found himself imagining the mess they'd make if they were unlucky enough to encounter a speeding bus while cutting through an intersection. The bus would be unable or unwilling to stop, he knew. The family would go flying. There would be a flurry of recriminations, shouts, tears. As if out of nowhere, some municipal authorities would eventually appear to clean it all up. And more than a billion people, one sixth of humanity, would get on with their lives.

He was still thirsty.

Knowles did not often act on impulse: certainly not in his business dealings. But a cold drink was a cold drink, so long as the bottle was properly sealed, and he was unwilling to wait until they reached the hotel. Leaning forward slightly, leather upholstery squeaking beneath the tailored tropical silk of his trousers, he murmured to the driver.

"I need a cold drink, Raju. Pull over someplace."

While startled by the request, the chauffeur did not look back at his important passenger. Though a poor man, the driver believed he enjoyed a fortunate life. To take one's eyes off traffic while driving in an Indian city was to invite suicide.

"*Here*, sir?"

Amused by the man's response, Knowles glanced briefly to his right, out the tinted window. "Yes, here. Why not? The drinks for sale here come from the same plant as the ones at the hotel, don't they?"

"Yes, sir. I suppose so, sir. Please, just let me find a good place."

"Any place will do. Any stand." Knowles leaned back against the cushioning seat. He was enjoying himself.

At least, he was until the driver finally settled on one of the hundreds of tiny clapboard street-side stands, most of which were smaller than the bathroom in the suite at the executive's hotel, pulled over, got out, and opened the passenger-side door of the Mercedes. It was as if a door had been opened to a commercial oven. But having made the suggestion and forced the issue, Knowles felt compelled to brazen it out.

Even though he did nothing more strenuous than get out of the car, he began perspiring immediately. He could feel the clammy droplets drip-dripping from his armpits down his sides. Well, he had intended to change as soon as he got back to the hotel anyway. A dip in the pool would fix everything.

The man behind the battered, splintered wooden plank that served as a counter front for the cubicle was slender and active. You expected both in India. Everyone was attuned to business as a way of life, and there were very, very few fat people. There was no sidewalk, of course. Where the cracked and abused asphalt layer of the street ended, dirt began. Cut by occasional rivulets and rills, what passed for the space between the road and the first tattered buildings was paved only with garbage, rocks, and pieces of flaked roadbed. Even the plastic and paper litter looked hot.

Efficient and expectant, the cubicle keeper inquired of the driver as to his customers' needs. While the chauffeur ordered, the several locals who were hanging out looked up from their seats at one of the two tables that had been set out on the dirt and gazed with unapologetic interest at the tall European. Such directness was another Indian trait. If they thought he spoke any Hindi, Knowles knew, within minutes they would openly be asking him the intimate details of his life; everything from did he have children to how much did he make in a year.

Raju came back with a pair of cool, if not cold, Fantas. While Knowles sipped his, after carefully wiping off the rim, he contemplated the endless parade of animals and humanity that overflowed the overworked street as thoroughly as floodwaters ever filled a riverbed. The current parted only for a pair of Brahma cows. Chewing their cuds while seated serenely in the middle of traffic, they ignored the lethal hysteria swirling all around them, secure in holy bovine confidence that everything from lurching cement trucks to rampaging interstate buses would swerve to miss them. And in truth, there was not so much as a scratch on hindquarter or flank. Of all the thousands of sacred steers Knowles had encountered on his many visits to the subcontinent, he had yet to see one that had been injured by a vehicle.

The beggar did not seem to step out of the human current so much as appear before him. He was of average height, about five foot six, and clad in dirty but intact cotton pants and overshirt. Stained as if by coal, his feet were unshod. Though uncut and hanging almost to his shoulders, his straight black hair had been given a cursory combing. The face was lean and undistinguished, the nose slightly hooked. Higher up, black eyes stared unblinkingly at Knowles. The man's right hand was extended toward him, palm open and facing up, in a pose familiar since humanity began.

Knowles ignored him. It was what you had to do, he felt. Giving the man money would only serve to instantly draw a crowd, and the executive had not yet finished his drink. He turned away. Not condescendingly, but just enough to show he was uninterested.

The beggar stayed, hand out, eyes fixed, staring. The index finger rose. One rupee, the man was saying silently. About two cents at current exchange rates, Knowles knew. It didn't matter. It wasn't the money. It was the principle of the thing. The man looked healthy enough, especially compared to some of the pitiful specimens the executive had seen. Agra was a reasonably prosperous place. There was work to be had. Knowles believed it was his responsibility not to encourage the fellow.

At least he was being quiet about it. Nothing more aggressive than the politely upraised index finger. But the unbroken stare was growing unnerving. Irritated now, Knowles turned further away and muttered, *"Nahi, nahi."*

The man could not or would not take the hint. He remained where and as he was; silent, persistent, demanding. While clearly uneasy, the chauffeur was reluctant to intervene. Not so the shopkeeper. Carrying the pan of soapy water with which he had been scrubbing his walls and few dishes, he came out from behind his makeshift counter and began yelling at the beggar. While Knowles could not follow the rapid stream of annoyed Hindi, it was clear enough what the shopkeeper was saying. Get lost, and quit bugging my customers.

The beggar ignored him, his unswerving, unbroken stare reserved solely for the well-dressed European. Knowles drank a little faster. The man was ruining the small pleasure of the cold drink.

There was a sudden loud, almost shocking splash as the shopkeeper heaved the filthy contents of the dishpan. The dirty water struck the beggar square in the face. For the first time, his eyes closed and he twitched slightly. Behind Knowles, the cruel laughter of the slightly better-off came from the men seated at the table. The beggar's black eyes opened and shut a couple of times as he blinked away the wastewater. Otherwise he hardly moved. Displaying either maniacal determination or immense natural dignity, he remained where he was, the arm still outstretched, never having wavered even when he had been struck by the water. The index finger remained upraised. One rupee. Two cents.

With the eyes of the now amused men at the table following him, Knowles handed the empty soda bottle to the chauffeur, who returned it to the still irritated shopkeeper. The executive let himself back into the car, careful not to burn his fingers on the door. As chilled air enveloped him and the car started to pull slowly back out onto the pavement, he saw the vagrant outside the window. The man was bent over and staring in at him, expectant palm hovering outside the tinted glass. The beggar followed like that until the car accelerated slightly and entered traffic.

Knowles never looked back. His thoughts were already elsewhere. He had automatically put the encounter with the possibly deranged panhandler out of his mind.

Within the grand lobby of the high-rise, five-star hotel, men and women of many nationalities promenaded freely. Sikhs sporting tightly wound, multi-colored turbans discussed business with visitors from opposite sides of the world while Indian women draped in sarees of brilliantly colored silk and gold thread flowed frictionlessly across thick woolen carpets from Tibet. Laughing and giggling, several innocent children of the privileged chased each other in the direction of the hotel pool.

Knowles hesitated as he approached the gold-colored elevators. Work and the subsequent drive back to the hotel had made him hungry. Not hungry enough for a meal. A proper dinner was still hours away. But a quick snack would be nice.

The hotel boasted a fine bakery. Entering and finding himself alone, he scanned the contents of the wood and glass cases while waiting for the absent attendant to put in an appearance. The slick sugary sheen of freshly chilled Napoleons and dark chocolate éclairs was tempting enough, but he had learned from previous trips to develop a taste for the fine local sweets. He decided on a quarter kilo of small rectangles of dense pastry made with a dough of semolina flour and finely ground cashew nuts that had been sweetened with Lebanese honey and rose syrup.

Where was the attendant? Sensing slight movement behind him, he turned from inspecting the high-caloric contents of the display cases, and nearly stumbled with shock. Staring back at him was not the attendant, but the unblinking beggar who had accosted him outside the roadside stand. Black eyes bored into the executive's own. The open palm extended toward him.

This was disgraceful, an outraged Knowles felt. There was no way on Earth such a vagabond ought to have been able to slip into the hotel past its intense and ever watchful security. Evidently a staff that was not ever watchful, he decided angrily. He would have a few harsh words for the management, harsh words indeed!

"*Nahi!*" he barked furiously as he pushed past the man. Though the brief physical contact was rough, even challenging, the beggar did not respond, either with word or gesture. Instead, he simply turned and followed Knowles, tracking the executive with open palm and unblinking eyes.

When he was halfway to the elevators, Knowles turned to look back. To his relief, the beggar was gone. Not surprising, the executive decided. If the man had any sense at all, if he knew what was good for him, he would already have slipped out of the hotel by whatever mysterious means he had sneaked in. It was unconscionable to think such individuals could make their way into a hotel of this class. Perhaps the next time he visited Agra, Knowles decided, he would take his trade elsewhere.

He was debating whether to return to the bakery when the elevator arrived. The hell with it, he decided. He would order something from room service.

The latter was so prompt and so good and the waiter who brought it to the room so politely obsequious that Knowles magnanimously decided to forget the letter of complaint he had composed in his mind. A swim followed by a fine dinner in the hotel's main restaurant settled him further into a state of general contentment. Tomorrow he would be off anyway, back to London, the contract signed to his satisfaction. He was looking forward to escaping from the appalling heat and poverty and getting back to real civilization.

It was while coming out of the shower that he nearly bumped into the beggar.

Knowles was not a man easily frightened. He was used to commanding, to giving orders, and to having them obeyed. He was also physically much bigger than the lean whip of visibly undernourished intruder. The man was between him and the door. A second door accessed the hall from the sitting room of the suite. If he broke and ran for it, would this insane intruder chase him and try to stop him? A thought made the executive suddenly nervous. Was his unwanted visitor armed? Even beggars could afford a cheap knife.

But there was no threat in the man's open, staring eyes. Only a silent demand reinforced by the open palm and the upraised index finger. One rupee. Damn the bastard! Knowles would not give in. It was a matter of principle. The letter of complaint he had intended to write to hotel management returned in full fury. Bad enough the transient had managed to sneak into the hotel. For him to find his way upstairs, to Knowles's very room, was inexcusable. Turning, he started for the sitting room.

The beggar moved to block his path.

For the first time, Knowles found himself growing slightly concerned. There was still no sign of a weapon, but who knew what a madman like this was capable of doing? Retreating slowly, never taking his eyes off the intruder, he considered picking up the phone and dialing security. Ordinarily, the gesture alone would be enough to frighten off any intruder. Any sane intruder, the executive reminded himself.

"Get out of here," he snapped as he backed away. Who knew what possibly contagious diseases lurked within those soiled cotton garments? Was the room already infected with something unseen? He felt the wall and window bump up behind him. Arm outstretched, the man continued to approach. True to form, he had still not uttered a word. A small piece of garbage from the dirty dishwater the shopkeeper had thrown in his face still clung to his left cheek.

Enough, Knowles decided. This was going to stop, and it was going to stop here and now. And if the hotel could not do its job, well, he would damn well have to do it for them. Balling his right hand into a tight fist, he drew back his arm.

And screamed as he felt the window vanish behind him.

"He fell."

Sergeant Tarun and Inspector Aggrawal studied the place on the pale pavement near the pool where the body had been found. Only the slightest hint of a stain remained, the hotel staff having scrubbed furiously at the spot all morning. Fortunately, the accident had occurred late at night, while the pool area was closed. Only one hotel guest had been disturbed, and that was the unfortunate woman out for an early morning swim who had discovered the body. Her hysteria had been cured by a clearing of her bill.

"But what was he doing on the roof?" Tilting back his head, the Inspector squinted up at where the sharp crest of the hotel intersected the haze-filled pre-monsoon sky. It was going to be hot today. It was going to be hot until July.

"Who says he was on the roof?" Kneeling, the sergeant studied the place of demise. The chalk that had been used to outline the broken, splattered remains of the corpse had long since been scoured away by the hotel staff.

"He had to have been on the roof." The Inspector was as confident in person as he had been in his report. "All the windows in this hotel are sealed and can only be opened with a special key, in the event of emergency or a breakdown in the air con system."

Sergeant Tarun straightened. "I expect we'll never know exactly what happened."

The Inspector nodded thoughtfully. "At least we can be sure it wasn't robbery. He had two hundred pounds, a hundred Euros, and four or five thousand rupees in his room."

"Lot of good it does him now." The sergeant looked up at his superior. "Chai?"

Aggrawal nodded. Stopping on the way back to the station for the traditional small cup of tea and milk, they were intercepted by a beggar. The woman had a babe in arms and a toddler at her feet, one finger shoved up its dirty nose. It regarded them out of innocent dark eyes that showed a spirit of curiosity that had not yet been crushed by life. The Inspector handed her a coin. He always kept a handful of small change in his pocket for just such encounters.

Besides being right, it was the sensible thing to do.

4 THE FROG AND THE MANTAS

I n 2004, I spent a month in the idyllic northern Pacific country of Palau. Though Palau has a population of only about 22,000, like most Pacific island countries it has a rich tradition of storytelling and mythology. In 2004 it was host to the Festival of the Pacific Arts. Held in a different oceanic country once every four years under the auspices of the SPC (Secretariat of the Pacific Community), it brings together the best painters, sculptors, tattoo artists, weavers, wood carvers, dancers, and singers for a two-week festival of fun and cultural exchange. It also, where feasible, brings together would-be writers.

To make a long story short, I ended up running the creative writing tranche of the Festival. The result was a handful of short stories based on Palaun legend, folklore, and life. Believing they were good enough to see print, I took them to the local SPC representatives. They agreed to publish them, as one of the achievements of the Festival. I expected the result would be a few dozen spiral bound xeroxed copies.

What eventuated, much to my astonishment, was an exquisite hardbound book titled Short Stories from Small Islands that featured a die-cut dust jacket, pressed flower endpapers, fine paper, and illustrations mimicking traditional Palauan storyboard woodcarving. Alas, both the English and French editions of the book sold out very quickly. The cover illustration reproduced a storyboard carving by master carver Ling Tinabu. My wife JoAnn collects frogs, there are plenty of frogs in Palau, and so I had Tinabu do a frog storyboard carving set in a manta-shaped frame.

I had no intention of writing a story for the collection. But after picking up the storyboard I had commissioned, I found myself a tad inspired by the result. I envi-

sioned myself sitting on a beach telling the ancient tale behind the carving to a cluster of attentive local youngsters. Sorry I can't show you the actual storyboard carving. You'll have to use your imagination.

Which is what stories like this are for....

Once upon a time, on the island of Babeldaob, in the country of Belau, there lived a tree frog named Baste. Of all the tree frogs, Baste was the most adventurous and brave. He was also very curious, and always eager to try new things.

Baste's favorite thing to do was to sit out on the longest branch of his favorite tree, which looked out over the great lagoon, and watch the mantas playing. "I wish I could fly through the water like that," he would say to himself. "But all I can do is hop, and kick."

Then one day it occurred to Baste that maybe if he practiced very, very hard, he might be able to swim swiftly through the water like the graceful mantas did. So, in secret and when the other frogs were not watching, because they surely would not have approved, he began to imitate the swimming motions of the mantas. Baste would stretch out his arms and legs as far as they would go, and spread his fingers and toes as wide as they would go, and flap them as hard as he could, just like the mantas flapped their wings underwater. He practiced and practiced.

And then one day, he was practicing so hard that he forgot to look where he was going, and he fell right out of the tree he was in, smack into the lagoon! Suddenly, he found himself in more water than he had ever been surrounded by in his life.

"What am I going to do now?" he thought anxiously. "I have only swam in small streams and pools, and here I am out in the very ocean itself."

Then a huge, beautiful shape came close behind him. Whirling frantically around in the water, he saw that it was a manta; perhaps one of the very mantas he had watched and admired for so long.

"Just what is it you think you're doing, frog?" the manta demanded to know.

"Please, sir—or missus," Baste replied (for it is very difficult to tell a Mr. Manta from a Mrs. Manta), "I've watched and envied you for so long, I thought that if I worked at it really hard, I could learn how to fly through the water just like you." While Baste was speaking, several other mantas had drifted close to see what was going on. After listening to the frog, they whispered awhile among themselves. Then the first manta, pivoting in the water like a ballet dancer, turned back to him.

"Well then, frog, if you have been trying for so long and so hard, let's see what you can do." And he swam away, with the other mantas joining him.

Baste hesitated. Then he screwed up his courage, and his face (which is an interesting thing to see in a frog) and just like he had been practicing, he began to flap his arms and his legs and his big webbed feet as hard as he could. And what do you know ... soon he was flying through the water alongside them, swimming just like a manta! He was extremely proud of his accomplishment, as well he should have been.

But soon he found himself beginning to fall further and further behind, for frogs are very small and mantas are very big and strong. Finally exhausted, he slowed to a stop in the water, stuck his head out, and waved. "Hey guys!" he shouted. "Wait up, wait up!"

But mantas have very small ears, and don't hear too well, and quickly they were out of sight.

Looking around, Baste saw that he was very far from the island that was his home, and even farther from the nearest tree. He began swimming; not like a manta this time, for he was quite tired, but like a frog—kick, kick, kick. After a while, he sensed something following him, and turned, thinking it was one of his new friends, the mantas. But it was not a manta.

It was a silvertip shark.

Now, silvertips are very handsome sharks, very sleek and graceful. But Baste didn't think the silvertip was handsome at all. In fact, he thought it was pretty scary-looking.

"Hullo," rumbled the very interested silvertip. "What have we here? Why, it's a frog. And so far from shore, too." He swam a little closer and smiled. When a shark smiles, it doesn't mean he's amused. It means—something else. "I do believe I'm going to eat you, little frog."

Baste looked around frantically, but out in the lagoon there was no tree to hide behind, no roots to burrow beneath, no big green leaves to pull over his head. He was all alone, and he knew that no matter how hard he had practiced swimming like a manta, he could not outswim a silvertip shark.

"Please, sir!" he squeaked, "I'm only a frog. Hardly a mouthful for such as you."

"That's all right," replied the silvertip easily. "I'm kind of in the mood for just a little snack, anyway." And smiling very wide indeed, he moved closer to the terrified Baste.

Just then a shadow appeared beneath them both—and then another, and another. Soon seven giant mantas had gathered around the frog and the shark, and were glowering warningly at the silvertip. Now, mantas have no teeth, and ordinarily a silvertip shark would not be afraid of a manta. But *seven* mantas can weigh as much as seven tons. The silvertip thought about it, and decided the possible fight wasn't worth a fast bite, and swam off quietly, muttering to himself and not smiling anymore.

"Thank you!" Baste told them, letting out a long, deep sigh of relief. "Thank you, oh, thank you for saving me!"

"You're welcome," sang a voice as deep and mysterious as the sea itself.

The biggest manta came forward, the tips of his vast wings seeming to put half the lagoon floor in shadow. He was very old, and very wise. Having been around the lagoon a time or two, he knew a few things about the way the world was, and ought to be. He looked at the little frog out of understanding eyes.

"I think, frog, that maybe you should stick to the trees, and the fresh-water streams, and the rainwater pools, and leave the manta-ing to those of us who were born to it," he murmured kindly.

"I will do just that," a relieved Baste assured him, still looking around nervously from time to time. "But how can I get back onto the island? There is no beach here, and the sides of the rocks are very steep."

"We can take care of that," the old manta told him. "Swim out onto the tip of my wing, right there."

Baste did as he was told, and with a flip of its powerful wing, the manta launched the frog just like a rocket straight toward the nearest bunch of trees. For a long moment, Baste was *really* flying. He landed in a clump of pandanus leaves, rolled over once, got up, and immediately scrambled up onto the nearest branch. There he sat, licking himself with his long tongue, drying in the sun, and thinking about what a close call he'd had.

From that day on, Baste never tried to go swimming with the mantas again. But he would still sit in his favorite tree on the branch that over-hung the clear water, and watch them leaping and playing in the lagoon. And every once in a while, when none of the other frogs were looking, he would flap his arms and legs really, really hard, and instead of hopping, fly a short way to the next nearest tree.

5 MR. DEATH GOES TO WASHINGTON

I wrote this after seeing a number of pictures of the Vietnam Memorial in Washington, DC. What more natural, I thought, than that Death himself should put in an appearance at such a place? But what would he be doing there? Reminiscing? Mourning? Chortling?

Maybe it was just a coincidence that he should find himself in such a place, for essentially unrelated reasons. Just as the heroine of the story. They meet, but what then? Their encounter has to relate to the location, but how and in what way?

For that I am indebted to the inspiration provided by the greatest (my opinion) writer of short speculative fiction, the inimitable Robert Sheckley. You might look up his short story "The Accountant."

Unlike in most fantasy, every word of Melody's spells is real, and lifted unabridged from the world's greatest source of enervating spellcasting....

Perhaps unsurprisingly, Melody encountered Mr. Death at the memorial to the veterans of the Vietnam War. He was standing there staring at the smooth, polished black wall, studying the inscribed names as if a relative of his own had been memorialized thereon. In a sense, they were all his relatives. He had not killed any of them; no, not a one. But he had taken them all; lo, every one.

She recognized him immediately, of course. Death is a hard entity to miss, even on a late winter's day in the nation's capital. There were plenty of ordinary folk about who trailed behind them the aspect or aroma of death. They entered or emerged from buildings that were heavily if cunningly guarded, and to which a teenage visitor and would-be political intern like Melody Johannsen from Minnesota was denied access. Being sensitive, and unusually schooled, she was able to recognize many of these people. Not only because they could not shake from their spirits the unpleasant odor of death and dying, but because they usually had the fashion sense of a catwalk of slugs.

Death himself, now—that was another matter of matter indeed.

Her widowed mother had always taught her to be straightforward and curious. "Doing nothing is safe, but that's not how you learn about the world." Melody was not afraid of Death. He looked like a lonely old man, albeit one badly in need of a good home-cooked Midwestern meal. He was tall and slender, with a mournful expression, but far from intimidating in appearance. He wore, as one would have imagined, a black suit, though from the cut of it she could not tell if it was a casual outfit meant for daily wear or a uniform. None of the other people who were wandering slowly back and forth in front of the memorial, many of them sobbing quietly, noticed him. Perhaps, in a place of death, Death himself is harder for most people to distinguish.

More likely, identification came easy to her because Melody was a sorceress.

Well, to be entirely truthful, an apprentice sorceress. They were scarce in Minnesota, though shamans were plentiful. Being of Swedish descent, her source for serious sorceressness was Norse, arising from the myth and mystery of ancient Scandinavian legend, of the doings of great gods and goddesses. Melody was blond and very pretty, but no goddess. Not even the boys on the football team who kept trying to date her thought that, though some of their false compliments approached it in presumption.

Thanks to her mother's patient instruction, Melody had gumption, if not presumption. So after watching the lanky figure inspect the sweeping black stone litany of loss for several minutes, she took a slightly deeper breath than usual, walked up to him, and as soon as she had attracted his attention, inquired straightforwardly but not innocently, "What are you doing here?"

Death looked down at her and smiled. It was not an attractive smile, but it was tolerable. Although it might well have set a non-sorceress (all right, just an apprentice) to screaming.

"I beg your pardon?"

Taking the notion that Death might beg anyone's pardon as encouragement, she pressed on. "You're Death, and I'm interested to know what you're up to here in the capital on this very fine day in March."

The smile widened slightly, but became no more pleasant. She took no umbrage. It wasn't his fault, she knew. We are who (and what) we are. "You are a very insolent young woman. I am Martin Mulvaney, of 435 East Delaware Way, in Chevy Chase. Apartment 8B."

"You may very well live at 435 East Delaware in Chevy Chase. No one knows where Death abides. At least, not on a daily basis. Besides, I'm from out of town and I don't know the local neighborhoods. But I am sure that you are not Martin Mulvaney, or any of the Mulvaney clan. You are Death."

The angular shape looked around, craning to see if anyone was watching them. No one was. Everyone else's attention was on loved ones, be they living or memorialized in marble. He turned back to the girl confronting him, and this time there was a depth and a darkness to his eyes into which a careless soul could plunge and drown.

"If I am Death, then shouldn't you be a little afraid of me?"

"Why should I be afraid of you? You're a component of everyday life, as natural and as a part of it as the air and the water. I wasn't raised to be afraid of Death, though I really never thought I'd get to meet him. At least, not until time."

The polite smile turned to a disapproving frown. "I am no entertainment celebrity, to be gawked at and casually mocked."

"Am I being flippant?" she inquired.

He pursued his lips, which when he did so turned very, very white. "No, you are not being flippant. I perceive, somewhat to my astonishment, that you are being quite serious, as well as friendly and respectful. Respectful is advisable." The voice dropped to a dangerous rumble that hinted of dimensions unknown. "Friendly is dangerous."

"I'm not afraid of you," she repeated unflinchingly. Cocking her head slightly to one side, she eyed him intently. "You don't look like what I'd imagined."

"A lot of people say that. Just before the end." That grim smile again. "The face of Death is not blank. My job isn't to scare people. Quite the contrary. I dislike a fuss. My work is taxing enough as it is." He leaned toward her then, and Melody found she could smell him. Like his appearance, it wasn't especially foul. Not when it was this fresh, anyway. She had an aunt in St. Paul whose attic smelled much the same.

"You're charming and pretty and bold," Death told her. "Would you be interested in coming to work for me? Good help is always hard to find."

"No thanks," she replied. "I already have enough homework. I want to come to work here one day and represent my state. I want to be a Senator and help people."

"Oh dear," he hissed softly. "We'll be seeing a lot of each other, then." As if that concluded the conversation, he turned away from her.

Absently, she noted that he cast no reflection in the wall of polished black marble. That was to be expected from a specter. "Why are you here?" she asked quickly, repeating her initial question before he could fade to a shade.

He paused and turned back to her, his expression a knowing scowl. "You really are an intrepid little girl."

"I'm not a little girl," she snapped. "I'm fifteen."

A different sort of smirk this time: still ominous, but also slightly wistful. "I am somewhat older. Listen to me, um, young lady: you'd best mind your own business. Even though it's not your prescribed time, I am allowed a certain leeway in these matters." He inhaled audibly, but not of air. "Since you seem determined to discover that which you would be better off not knowing, my purpose in being here is to pick up a number of people." Turning, he raised an arm and pointed. "In a short while there's going to be quite a dramatic crash just over that way involving a pair of tour buses going too fast in opposite directions. By coincidence, I believe that several elderly couples from your state are on board one of the vehicles. For a moment or two thereafter I expect to be quite busy."

Death's remorseless description of what was poised to ensue did not upset her. It was his indifference that got her small-town dander up.

"No," she said.

It's not easy to surprise Death, but she succeeded. Heavy eyebrows rising, he eyed her evenly. *"No?"*

"No." She made sure her purse was securely slung over her shoulder, the better to keep her hands free. "I have nothing against death in the course of things, but I'm dead set against these kinds of unnatural tragedies. Especially when one of my possible future constituents may be involved."

"Dear me," Death murmured sardonically. "Should I be afraid? What are you going to do if I proceed? Kill me?" Death might not be proud, but he was affluent with irony.

"Stop you," she replied calmly. "If I'm going to be a worthy Senator, I have to be able to stop bad things from happening."

The pale death's-head nodded slowly. "A sensible observation. In that case, I suggest you prepare to begin with protecting yourself. As I am not constituted to brook any interference in my work, I expect I'd better start this afternoon's work with you." He glanced briefly southward again. "I have a little time yet." And with that, he extended a long, skinny arm in her direction, the fingers of the hand opening toward her like the white grapples of a cargo crane. One touch of those cold, cold digits, and she would pass immediately and irrevocably from the realm of the living.

No one seemed to be looking in their direction. It was as if the two contending figures had suddenly entered into an isolated pocket of reality where only they existed: Melody Johannsen, of Remsburg, Minnesota (pop. 2,342, and static), and Death, of the Hereafter (pop. unknown, and ever-growing). Remembering everything she had studied over the past several years in the course of her desire to become a Senator as well as maintain her family tradition, she raised both arms high, inclined her fingers forward, and proceeded to intone with solemn force.

"An objection may be made to the consideration of any original main motion, and to no others, provided it is made before there is any debate or before any subsidiary motion is stated. Thus, it may be applied to petitions and to communications that are not from a superior body, as well as to resolutions. It cannot be applied to incidental main motions, such as amendments to by-laws, or to reports of committees on subjects referred to them."

The reaching claw of a hand halted, the grasping fingers stopping more than a foot from the front of her neatly starched blouse. Death blinked. A bemused expression came over his face. It took a few seconds and a violent shake of his head to clear the cobwebby enchantment from his mind. Any suggestion of a smile had vanished from his face, that now assumed a thoroughly grave and grim expression. It was the look of imminent demise, of incipient destruction, that would brook no turning. Once more, he reached for her.

Holding her ground, Melody modulated her tone so that it became as monotonous, as boring, as entirely enervating a dreary drone as could be produced by the otherwise captivating human voice. One could properly and accurately call it deadly dull. It was almost—congressional.

"Incidental motions are such as arise out of another question which is pending, and therefore take precedence of and must be decided before the question out of which they rise; or, they are incidental to a question that has just been pending and should be decided before any other business is taken up. They yield to privileged motions, and generally to the motion to lay on the table. They are undebatable, except an appeal under certain circumstances as shown in section 21. They cannot be amended except where they relate to the division of a question, or to the method of considering a question, or to methods of voting, or to the time when nominations or the polls shall be closed. No subsidiary motion, except to amend, can be applied to any of them except a debatable appeal. Whenever it is stated that all incidental motions take precedence of a certain motion, the incidental motions referred to are only those that are legitimately incidental at the time they are made. Thus, incidental motions take precedence of subsidiary motions, but the incidental motion to object to the consideration of a question cannot be made while a subsidiary motion is pending, as the objection is only legitimate against an original main motion just after it is stated, before it has been debated or there has been any subsidiary motion stated."

Letting out a cry of pain, Death staggered backward. For a third time he raised his hands—only now they were employed not in trying to reach her, but to cover his ears. If it had not been Death uttering it, the cry of pain expressed by the tall figure would have been truly pitiable. Following up her advantage, Melody advanced relentlessly, lowering her arms and shaking one finger portentously at the gaunt figure that was trying to stumble away from her.

"Furthermore," she continued while channeling the implacable insensitivity of only the most accomplished parliamentarians, "the motion to suspend the rules may be made at any time when no question is pending; or while a question is pending, provided it is for a purpose connected with that question. It yields to all the privileged motions (except a call for the orders of the day), to the motion to lay on the table, and to incidental motions arising out of itself. It is undebatable and cannot be amended or have any other subsidiary motion applied to it, nor can a vote on it be reconsidered, nor can a motion to suspend the rules for the same purpose be renewed at the same meeting except by unanimous consent, though it may be renewed after an adjournment, even if the next meeting is held the same day."

"Stop, stop!" Unable to take any more, Death threw the back of one forearm across his eyes and turned away. There was a blast of noisome air, like the collapsing of a balloon, and then he was gone.

Aware that at least one passing couple was now staring in her direction, Melody lowered her arms to her sides, adopted a look of small-town innocence, and headed for the memorial's east exit. No one paid any attention to her as she departed. She had arranged to meet her mother back at the hotel in time for lunch. The recent confrontation would provide food for thought, and she was sure her mother would have both reprimands and suggestions to make. From somewhere not far south of the memorial, there was a screeching of brakes as one fully loaded tour bus swerved violently to just miss another entering the intersection from the opposite direction. The occupants of both vehicles continued on their way, blissfully unaware of how close many of them had just come to having their visit to the nation's capital shockingly and lethally terminated.

North of them and closer to the capitol building, one of the state of Minnesota's future Senators, and most accomplished (apprentice, 2nd class) sorceresses, made sure to look both ways before crossing the street on the way back to her hotel. True to her word, she had done her homework well. While proud of that, she was not one to rest on her laurels, however accomplished. Prevailing over Death had been easy enough.

Getting something that would actually help people through Congress was going to require a great deal more knowledge, both legislative and sorceral, than she had managed to master to date.

6 FOOD FIGHT

When an editor requests a story, sometimes you have to work hard to come up with an idea suitable for the designated anthology. Then you struggle to expand the idea into an actual story. The process can be time-consuming and more than a little frustrating.

Other times, the idea just materializes. BANG! an import from that other dimension some refer to as the creative consciousness. Or cortex. I'm not sure which. All I know is that this story came zooming in on demand, arising out of a common phrase most often utilized by restaurant critics and a bit of knowledge about representatives of the opposite gender. I hope the latter doesn't get me in trouble.

It never has....

"My coffee keeps insulting me."

Dr. Erin Alderfield flicked a glance to her left to make sure the recorder light was still on, scratched unobtrusively at the place on her slim neck where the thin gold necklace she was wearing never seemed to sit quite right, tilted her head downward so she could look over the wire brim of her glasses, and thoughtfully regarded her patient. Seated on the couch across from her, Morton Ropern pushed nervously at the front of his forehead where twenty years earlier he used to have a good deal more hair and waited for the therapist to respond.

It did not take long. "Mr. Ropern, coffee does not talk. Coffee has no body, no organic physicality, and therefore no brain, much less larynx, lungs, and tongue. It is a liquid: nothing more, nothing less, sometimes imbibed chilled, more often hot. It cannot talk."

Far from being dissuaded by this bracing dose of cold realism, Morty Ropern's reply spilled out (so to speak) even faster than before. "And it isn't just the coffee. It's the cream, the sugar, and the bagel I have that usually accompanies it every morning." He hesitated. "For some reason, the onion tends to keep quiet." While still somewhat south of frantic, his expression could at least be said to be verging decidedly on the fretful. "Dr. Alderfield, what I am going to *do*?" The slight but trim forty-year-old looked anxiously around the neat, bookshelf-heavy office. "No matter where I am anymore, food *talks* to me."

Dr. Alderfield checked the recorder again. Usually each day at work was much like another, every patient similar to the one who preceded or followed. Not today. Not this patient. She was beginning to scent the rapidly expanding zygote of an incipient scientific paper.

"Does all food talk to you?" she inquired with admirable solicitude, "or just breakfast?"

"All food, everywhere." Inordinately relieved not to have had his phobia dismissed out of hand (much less with derisive laughter), Ropern worried on. "And not just my food. Other people's food, too. Food in supermarkets, food in convenience stores. Sometimes I just overhear it talking to itself, but more often than not lately it recognizes something in me and addresses itself directly to me."

Perhaps it senses a kindred flakiness, Dr. Alderfield found herself thinking, though she of course said nothing of the kind. "I see." Turning slightly to her right, she nodded in the direction of the wood-grained cabinet that dominated the far wall. "Behind that lower door is a small refrigerator. Inside are various cold drinks, water, and some small snacks." She returned her attention to her patient. "Is any of it, um, communicating with you now?"

Ropern looked in the indicated direction. Somewhat to Alderfield's surprise (and professional delight), the patient did not hesitate. "Mostly it's all chatting among itself. But there's a half-gallon container of orange juice whose drink-by date expired two weeks ago, and it wants me to tell you that it's pissed."

Profession and experience aside, Dr. Alderfield was also human. This response from her patient compelled her to, if not actually bite her tongue, to clamp her lightly glossed lips tightly together and for a moment turn her head away from him. When she had once more sufficiently composed herself, she looked back.

"I didn't realize that food could have, um, feelings."

Ropern's gaze met hers unflinchingly. "It hates waste."

"I see." She sat back in her chair, crossing legs that were shapely from decades of competition track, then city jogging. "How does it feel about being consumed?"

"Fulfilled," the patient responded immediately. He looked away, toward the window that opened out onto the noisy canyon of glass and steel towers. She recognized his expression immediately: it was the look of a patient suddenly wondering what he was doing in her office. "As far as I know, I'm the only one who can hear food talking."

She nodded reassuringly, then asked the question that could not be avoided. "I'm sure that is a condition that can be dealt with, given time and proper therapy. What I need to know now is—do you talk back?"

Guilt and embarrassment vied for control of his facial muscles. In the end, it was a draw. "I try not to, but sometimes I have no choice."

"Really?" It was not the expected response. But then, nothing about this case was expected. "It becomes a compulsion, then?" Mentally, she revised the prescription she had already intended to write for him.

"No, not a compulsion." Rising, Ropern began to pace the office. Sensing his nervousness, she let him roam at will. Purposefully, the room contained no sharp or edged objects. "For example, yesterday I was walking to work and I passed a guy eating the biggest, greasiest, grossest hamburger you ever saw. A real mess-on-a-bun. I could overhear the ingredients conspiring."

"'Conspiring?'" It was becoming harder and harder for her to maintain her professional aplomb in the face of such continuing, albeit inventive, illogicality.

Ropern, however, was dead serious. "The cheese was whispering to the meat patties and they were both conniving with the sauce. The onions and pickles tried to take a stance against them, but they didn't have a chance."

"I see. A chance to do what?"

"Help the poor slob. The cheese was murmuring, 'We're gonna kill this guy. His cholesterol's gotta be approaching four hundred. Let's push him over the edge.'" Ropern stopped pacing so abruptly that for just an instant Alderfield was alarmed. But his tone and manner were so subdued that she was quickly reassured. This patient's mania was not dangerous: only bizarre.

"Have you ever felt yourself similarly threatened?" she heard herself inquiring.

"Oh sure, plenty of times," Ropern assured her. "Usually by the same kinds of fatty, unhealthy foods. They're pretty transparent in their intentions."

"You're lucky," she told him. "Most people have to resort to reading nutritional charts."

"I don't feel lucky," he replied morosely. "I feel isolated, alone, and put-upon. I can't shut out the racket. Everywhere I go it's food, food, food everywhere, and all of it yammering away like a crowd at a football game." He glanced up sharply again. "A friend suggested I see you, but I really don't think I'm crazy."

"Of course you're not." Her voice was soothing, comforting. Practiced. "You're—perceptive. It's the exact nature of your perception that we have to define, and deal with."

That brought forth the first smile he had shown since checking in with her receptionist. "You're very understanding, Dr. Alderfield. My friend said you were understanding."

She shrugged off the compliment. "It's my job to understand. And to help those people who come to me to understand themselves, the world around them, and how they fit into it." Looking down, she checked her watch. "We can delve further into understanding, but not anymore today. Can you come back Friday, around ten in the morning?"

"I'll make time," he told her. A hand thrust out as he rose and came toward her. She did not flinch. The fingers enveloped one of her hands and shook it gratefully. "I feel better already. I've been carrying this around inside me for so long. Just being able to talk to someone about it is an enormous help." His eyes darting in the direction of the concealed refrigerator, he looked suddenly uneasy again. "I can't talk to food about it, of course."

"Of course," she agreed readily. "Friday, then." She nodded firmly toward the door. "My receptionist Mary-Elizabeth will give you a reminder card."

He started to exit, paused at the doorway to look back. "You're so accepting. I don't suppose you've ever had any food talk to *you*?"

She smiled. "One time in Zurich I had a peach melba call to me, but that's about the only occasion I can recall."

Wholly overlooking the gentle sarcasm, he nodded knowingly. "Desserts are the worst. They have this bad habit of always shouting." Then he was out the door and gone.

What a refreshing, and fascinating, change of pace, she thought as she walked over to the refrigerator to get something to drink. A patient who wasn't in love with his mother, didn't want to murder his boss, was confident in his chosen sexuality, and presented no immediate apparent danger to himself or to anyone else. On the other hand, his was the most purely wacky mania she had encountered in fifteen years as a practicing professional. As she plucked a glass off the shelf and opened the door to the small fridge, she was already composing the first paragraphs of the paper she intended to write.

Cold shock coursed down her front from chest to feet as the bottom fell out of the container and a quart of orange juice spilled down her suit to run down her legs. Looking down in surprise, she could only stare as the sticky liquid began to pool up in her expensive shoes.

After finishing the day at the firm where he worked shuffling sales statistics for a major retailer, Morton Ropern decided to take the long route back to his apartment, detouring by way of the harbor walk. Usually he avoided it because of all the cafes and tourist shops selling seafood and such, but it was too nice an evening to terminate prematurely, and he felt strengthened by his session with the new therapist.

He found that for the first time in a long while he was able to ignore the mutterings of the cooked crabs that whispered darkly from atop hillocks of preserving ice. Clam chowder simmered expectantly, waiting for hungry imbibers. Cotton candy leered at passing visitors, while rows of fudge commented stolidly from within their window-mounted trays. Such food stalls and displays were always a problem for him, though nothing was worse than the occasional unavoidable visits he had to make to the supermarket. To most folk, buying food was a necessary chore. For him, it was akin to temporarily imprisoning a sympathetic eight-year-old in an animal shelter.

"Buy me!" the cans of soup would scream at him as he hurried past. He wasn't a big fan of soup, but he inevitably found himself shuttling one or two cans into his shopping cart just to shut them up. "Bread—man can't live without bread!" he would hear as he tried to make his way through the bakery section. "Eat us and the bullies at the beach won't kick sand in your face!" the steaks and chops chorused accusingly. The cacophony, the pleading, the endless demands were unrelenting and deafening. It was all he could do to escape with a basket containing the minimal necessities.

He didn't even dare to try and shop the imported foods aisle.

Restaurants were mildly less stressful. There was less competition for his attention and the food was invariably more refined. Not only the menu, but the dialogue. He had once managed to carry on a very civilized tête-à-tête with a plate of oysters Rockefeller before the last of them found its way down his gullet. Butter set on the table tended to leave him alone, reserving its banter exclusively for the accompanying bread rolls, while the respective components of a properly prepared main course vied for consumption and his attention with the utmost politeness.

"You first," the main course would invariably declaim to the vegetables.

"No, no, you first—you're the entrée," the assortment of squash, beans, and carrots would counter.

"Don't be silly—you'll get cold," the steak or fish or chicken would reply.

"Don't argue—I'll go." Leave it to a phlegmatic side dish of potato or rice to behave more sensibly than anything else on the table.

"You're all going," Morty Ropern would tell them. At least their incessant demanding chatter helped him to eat sensibly, compelling him to vary his intake without favoring one dish over another.

All of this and more he explained to the attentive Dr. Alderfield that Friday morning and on subsequent visits. She remained neither judgmental nor accusative, gently bringing him back to the subject at hand when he threatened to wander, prodding him for details when it appeared as if he was going to hold back. With each successive session he felt better and better. She noticed the change, too, until at the end of one visit she finally felt it was time to challenge him with the next step.

"Are you doing anything tomorrow night?"

"What?" His eyes widened slightly.

"Tomorrow night. Are you doing anything? Do you have any plans?"

"Plans, no, I—I thought I might take in a movie."

"Good." She made sure the recorder was off. "Then it's a date."

"A date?" He looked bemused. "Is that kosher? I mean, a therapist going out with one of their patients? I thought ..."

"You've seen too many reality television shows. This is not a specifically social occasion: it's all part of your therapy. A movie will be nice—after we've had dinner."

"Din—oh no." He rose from the couch. "I couldn't. I mean, it would be ..."

She interrupted him gently. "What? Frightening? Amusing? You're doing much better, Morty. You're not obsessing about culinary conversation anymore. Each time you come in, you end up talking more and more about other things. About aspects of your daily existence that don't involve gossiping food." She smiled encouragingly. "About the rest of life. I think it's time to take the next step." She implemented a deliberately exaggerated pout. "Or is it just that you don't want to be seen with me?"

"Oh no," he said quickly. "I mean, I find you quite attractive—for a therapist. Hell, that didn't come out right." A self-conscious grin partially compensated for the faux pas. "I'd be delighted to go out with you. To a concert, to the seaside—even to a movie. But dinner ..." Concern creased his face as he slowly shook his head. "I don't know."

"I do," she told him confidently. "You'll see. Another step forward in your progress. Tomorrow night, then." Rising, she ushered him toward the door. "We can meet at the snack bar downstairs and then go to a real restaurant. You like French?"

He nodded. "Most of the time. Not when it starts trying to convince me to start smoking again. There's nothing more annoying than a know-it-all main course."

He had high hopes, and dressed accordingly. It had been a while since he had been out on a serious date. Even though he expected it to be as much session as date, there was no denying the somewhat steely attractiveness of Dr. Alderfield and his anticipation at spending the evening with her. If only the food would cooperate. Perhaps she was more right than he suspected. Perhaps the only ones talking at their table would be the two of them.

No such luck.

It started, naturally enough, with the appetizers. Escargot he didn't mind. The sautéed snails usually kept their somewhat snooty chatter to themselves. But the garlic sauce that accompanied them was sputtering right from the start. Aware that she was watching him intently, he did his best to ignore the insults and queries the food kept flinging his way. He succeeded in disregarding the comments of the steaming snails as well as the frequent admonitions and repeated tut-tutting of the Caesar salad that followed.

The main course, however, defeated him.

He had chosen the blandest entrée on the menu: a simple, straightforwardly prepared coq au vin. Unless embellished, wine sauce rarely uttered more than a mumble, and any chicken dish tended to be sufficiently boring to ignore. But Erin (he could hardly spend the entire evening calling her "Dr. Alderfield," they both had decided) had ordered a fantastic veal smitane. When you put veal, mushrooms, and sour cream together, the result was bound to be a conversational as well as gastronomical free-for-all.

Even so, he did not lose control until she started to bring a particular forkful of the main dish toward her mouth.

"Don't eat that," he heard himself saying, much to his horror.

She paused. The evening had gone better than expected, validating her somewhat unorthodox invitation (unorthodox phobias required unorthodox therapies, she had decided). There had been no indication from her patient that the food that had been brought to their table and subsequently devoured by the both of them had voiced so much as a casual greeting. Until now.

Fork halfway to mouth she looked over at him, hesitated, and slowly lowered it back to her plate. "I beg your pardon, Morty? Why not?"

"It's mostly cartilage, with a bit of bone in the center. It'll go down, but it won't sit well." His eyes dropped, embarrassment reflected in his expression as well as his voice. "It—told me so."

She eyed the fork that was now resting on her plate. It looked like any other mouthful sliced from the entrée. "It told you so?"

He swallowed hard. "It started complaining as soon as you made the first slice. The rest of the cutlet is potentially gastronomically upsetting, and it's been monologuing about it. Loudly."

Loudly. "Morty, food makes the person who's *eating* it upset. It doesn't upset itself."

He looked miserable. "You've eaten the good half," he told her. "The rest is undercooked."

Her characteristic self-control shaken, she found that she was growing angry. She firmly believed they had made a great deal of progress, and now he was just being—silly. Not a medically accurate description, perhaps, but an appropriate one. Sitting up straight, she brought the linen napkin to her mouth, dabbed delicately at her lips, and eyed him evenly. Sometimes therapy, especially in the field, required a directness that might be frowned upon if delivered in the office.

Deliberately, she raised the fork, bit off the bite-sized piece it held, chewed, and swallowed. Ropern looked quietly stricken.

She smiled back at him. "It's fine," she told him. After studying her plate, she sliced off another piece, divided it, and proceeded to down both halves. The sour cream-based sauce was delicious. She told him so.

"Well?" she prompted him. "What is my dinner saying now?"

"Nothing," he replied quietly. "But the peas and onions are lamenting the situation, while the au gratin is remaining determinedly neutral. Potatoes usually do."

She took a sip of the wine they had chosen. The only noise it made was as it slid refreshingly down her throat. "We've done a great deal of work together, Morton—Morty. Let's focus on the progress we've made. The last thing we want is regression." She eyed him sternly. "Food does not talk. Not my food, not your food. It doesn't tell you when it's safe or gone bad, it doesn't call out to you from greengrocer's stands, it doesn't fill your head with the kinds of inane inconsequentialities that allow the truly disturbed to set aside the real world in favor of some comforting imaginary one." Reaching across the table, she took his right hand in both of hers. Another bit of atypical therapy, but one she felt was vitally necessary at that moment.

"Does it?" she challenged him, her eyes locking onto his.

He paused. For longer than she would have wished. Just when she was starting to lose hope and thinking they might have to start all over again, from the beginning, a smile creased his face. It grew wider with every passing second.

"I—I guess not," he murmured. "Not if *you* say so."

Breakthrough. Not perfect and entire, but she would take it. Starting next week, they would build on it. Letting go of his hand, she sat back in her chair and took another sip of wine. Knife and fork dug into the remnants of her meal with gusto. She found she was looking forward to the after-dinner movie.

They let him ride with her in the back of the ambulance. He stayed with her all the way to the hospital. The appalled restaurant management not only comped the meal, including the wine, but paid for the transportation to the emergency room. They let him accompany her therein, too, and afterwards to the private room where she spent a restless, uneasy, stomach-churning night. Despite her intense discomfort, it was a night of revelations and further progress—though not of a kind she had anticipated.

Not long thereafter, friends were surprised to see them together on increasingly frequent occasions. They were even more surprised when she invited him to move in with her. No one was more startled at this than Morton Ropern himself. Not so much because of the invitation she smilingly proffered, but because he eagerly accepted.

"I don't see it," her best friend Miriam told her when they met for lunch the following week. "I mean, he has a good job and he's decent-enough looking and he isn't gay and he hasn't been married before, but really, Erin, he's no great catch."

Dr. Erin Alderfield munched on her salad. She looked, if not quite radiant, eminently content. "Morty has his special qualities. It's just that they're not all visible."

"Oh so?" The other woman was far from convinced. "Like what?" Seated at one of the café's sidewalk tables, she indicated the flow of humanity rushing to and fro nearby. "Tell me one thing I don't see that makes him such a special catch."

Erin looked up from her salad. "You should eat more fruit," she told her friend. "Good for the both of you." A secret smile caused her lips to part. "You could say that Morty's very good at foreign languages."

"For instance?" Miriam prodded her.

The look in her friend's eyes was distant, and glittering. "He can speak chocolate."

7 UNNATURAL

ny sufficiently advanced technology is indistinguishable from magic."
So declared Arthur C. Clarke, when he was not trouncing someone
like me at Ping-Pong. But what if the advanced technology was magic?
What if someone came along with another way of doing things that was so utterly
and completely different that it would be regarded as—what? An entirely new kind
of magic? A variation on same? Or something so utterly radical no one could
conceive of it before it actually was made reality?

Like employing lasers to play music instead of turning them into death rays?

I like to think that somewhere, some dreamer is lying abed envisioning an
utterly simple, straightforward, and dumbfoundingly easy way to go faster than
light by finding a way to avoid it.

This story is not about that.

The longer he stared at the battlefield map floating just above the massive
wooden table in front of him, the tighter grew the knot that had formed
in General Jaquard's stomach. He was not distracted from his study by the
distant baying of stabled wyverns, the howling of massed gryphons, and
the familiar reassuring crackle of evening cooking and cleaning spells.
Wholly absorbed in the most recently revised field map, he desperately
looked for surcease where there was none. Lying snug on his head and low
on his brow, the golden wreath of rank glowed an unsettling red,
reflecting his apprehension.

There was no denying the reality. The entire city was encircled and cut off. Desperate attempts by the defenders to break through the Misarian lines had been repeatedly rebuffed by the besiegers. A relief column sent in haste from the capital had failed to break through to the besieged. Propelled by anxiety and desperation, it had been ambushed by the enemy's fast wendigo cavalry and cut to pieces by lightning and wind. Though Tesselar was the harbor through which the majority of the Kingdom's goods passed, the disaster at Modrun Pass would force the government to think twice before attempting to relieve its garrison a second time. This had profound implications.

Foremost of which was the inescapable realization that the defenders of Tesselar were, essentially, now on their own. The responsibility for saving the city and therefore possibly the entire kingdom from the invading Misarians now fell on his shoulders. These were broad and strong, but at the moment, tired.

What could he do? Each day, the incantations that protected the citadel's walls weakened beneath the assault of relentless hexes cast forth by the attackers. Yesterday the South Gate had nearly splintered under a surprise late-night assault by a force of Misarian woodwraiths. Only the alertness of a certain Major Bolcapp in rushing up a squad of engineer forest sprites to rebond the wood fibers had prevented a potential disaster. For his speed and skill in responding to the unexpected attack, Bolcapp had been promoted Light Colonel. Posthumously, unfortunately. While directing the defense and repair of the gate, he had taken a choke curse above his protective body charm and had suffocated.

With the South Gate reinforced, the city remained safe. The surprise attack was but one more indication of the skill and stealthiness of the Misarian invader. There was no telling what cunning enchantment they might invoke next, what unimaginable force their general sorceral staff might pull from the depths of military conjuration. Jaquard did not feel overwhelmed. He was as adept at strategy as any senior officer the Kingdom's College of Martial Magic had ever graduated, and individually skilled as well. But he felt very alone.

Gryphons. If only he had more gryphons. More than ever, they were Tesselar's lifeline to the outside. Supply ships could not get through because of the Misarian's effective sea serpent and water sprite blockade of the harbor. Somehow, the city had to be relieved. Somehow, the siege had to be broken. It was clear now that after Modrun the government would be wholly occupied with marshalling its forces for the expected defense of the capital. He and his garrison were on their own.

It was at that moment that the bellspell attached to the door that led to his rooms appeared. It jangled apologetically next to his ear. Brushing it away, he turned irritably toward the entryway. It was after hours. Conscious of their commander's troubled state of mind, advisors and junior officers would know that at this time he would either be deep in thought or asleep and not to be disturbed. He muttered under his breath. An interruption this late likely meant another serious loss somewhere along the city wall. Waving a hand in the direction of the fireplace, he murmured an indifferent numinous word. The subdued flames within immediately responded, adding their additional light to the illumination from the drifting glowbulbs.

"Come in," he barked, "if you must."

He recognized the Captain. Petrone, his name was. Jaquard prided himself on knowing the names of every one of his junior as well as the senior officers. Petrone was a third-degree adept. To be promoted to a senior level, you had to be at least a seventh-degree. The man was old for a Captain. That might reflect as much on a lack of ambition as much as any ostensible paucity of skill.

While Petrone was old for a Captain, the officer who accompanied him looked young even for a junior lieutenant. Jaquard sighed internally. Were the Kingdom's forces spread so thin that the College been reduced to sending out ungraduated adepts? This—this *boy* ought to be at home with his parents, helping out with chores or reading books. Not preparing to sacrifice himself on the altar of national defense. He looked scarcely old enough to know how to cast a warming spell to heat his rations.

A reflexive, perfunctory glance at the lean lad's kit banished any empathy from the general's thoughts. The flickering light in the room further crevassed his frown.

"Soldier, where's your weapon?"

Automatically, the young officer glanced down in the direction of his empty holster. He swallowed hard. "I—I must have left it in my room, sir. I thought that since Captain Petrone and I were coming here, I didn't ..."

"Didn't need your wand?" Jaquard slapped his own holster. The heavy, powerful rod nestled snugly within responded by emitting an iris-shrinking blast of vertical light. "You're defending a city under siege whose attackers are inordinately clever and forever plotting. A soldier fighting under such circumstances should never be without his wand. Especially," he added sternly, "an officer."

"Yes sir, I'm sorry, sir." The lieutenant nervously shifted the beige cloth bag he was dragging from his left hand to his right.

Petrone stepped forward. Memories of supper and remnants of gravy flecked his beard, but Jaquard said nothing. In difficult circumstances, certain aspects of professional comportment had to be overlooked. Defending a city from looting and rapine allowed for different rules than when one was on parade.

"It's my fault, General. And I'm the one who insisted on coming here at this awkward hour." The old officer lowered his head slightly. "I thought it of vital importance that you see what this youngster has developed."

"Developed?" Jaquard was twice surprised. First to learn that the late-night interruption was not on behalf of the Captain but of his protégé, and second that such a callow-faced lieutenant might have something to contribute beyond stammer and shyness.

Petrone looked up at his commanding officer. Years seemed to drop away from him. "A matter of defense, sir. I was greatly skeptical when I first heard about it from other junior officers who had been witness to the headway. I was skeptical when I queried this young soldier about it." There was a flash in his eyes of something Jaquard had not seen in his troops for many days now. Hope? "I was skeptical, General, until I saw it for myself."

Petrone's demurral did nothing to reduce Jaquard's impatience. "Saw what, Captain?"

The old officer stepped aside. "Show him, Lt. Kemal."

Stepping forward, the lieutenant started to dump his heavy sack onto the stout wooden table, hesitated. "General, sir, is it ...?"

"Go ahead," Jaquard told him irritably. "Do whatever it is you have come to do." Turning his head, he glared meaningfully at Petrone. "This better not be a waste of my time. I'd say that it took you a considerable number of years to make captain. I wouldn't want for you to have to start over again." He shifted his penetrating gaze to the nervous but busy lieutenant. "Either of you." Petrone offered a wan but slightly defiant nod in return.

In the light from the huge stone fireplace and the hovering glowbulbs, the fledgling officer dumped out on the table a singular object. At first Jaquard thought, quite naturally, that it was some kind of modified wand.

It had the right general shape. But it was unusually large, nearly half his height, and festooned with additions he did not recognize. Though milled from honest wormwood, the handgrip, for example, bulged alarmingly at one end. Other odd protrusions were as unrecognizable as their purpose. Most of the wand, interestingly, appeared to consist of an iron tube.

"A two-handed wand," he commented as the lieutenant carefully laid other items out on the table. Perhaps he had been too hasty in reprimanding the younger officer. "Powerful I would assume, though not suited for close-quarter work."

Still arranging his adjunctives, the lieutenant spoke without looking up. "Begging your pardon, General, sir, but it's not a wand."

"Not a wand." Jaquard's frown returned. He studied the metal tube. "A pixie-duster, then."

"Not a pixie-duster." Was that a hint of a smile creasing Petrone's bewhiskered visage? "Sir."

"Well then, what the many devils regrettably not fighting on our side is it? Besides a waste of my time, soldier."

"I hope not that, General." The lieutenant picked it up. It did indeed require two hands to support. "It represents an interest of mine that has afflicted me since I was very young, but I've only just managed to make one work properly. It represents ..."

"A new way of looking at the world," Petrone could not resist putting in. "Perhaps even a new way of thinking about it."

What was all this nonsense? Philosophy? The Kingdom's Council was beridden with philosophers—none of whom could cast a fighting spell worth a lick. He said as much, utilizing language that would have seen him swiftly excused from Court.

"I call it a 'stun,'" the lieutenant said. "Because that's what it does."

"Ah." Jaquard relaxed, just a little. "It's a designated wand, then. For casting a stun spell."

Forgetting for a moment who he was talking to, the lieutenant looked exasperated. "No, sir, it's not a wand of any kind. It's something else. It's ..." he paused, finished rather lamely, "a 'stun.'"

"Show him," Petrone suggested hurriedly. Even in the dim light, he could see the color in the general's face darkening.

Nodding, Lieutenant Kemal set to work. First he dumped a small amount of a powder Jaquard did not recognize into a tiny pan positioned near the rear of the metal tube. The powder neither flashed nor smelled of even the simplest charm. From a small cloth bag, the lieutenant removed a thumb-sized ball of metal. That, at least, was immediately familiar to the general, whose sense of arcane smell was well-trained and highly sensitive. The ball was made of lead. He was not impressed. When it came to utilization for military incantations, lead was a notoriously ineffectual metal.

Tilting back the metal-and-wood contraption, the lieutenant proceeded to drop the lead ball into the metal tube. He followed it with a packet of ordinary, unenchanted cloth, ramming both deep into the tube with a long, thin piece of metal. This concluded, he stood cradling the tube in both arms, an air of readiness surrounding him. To the perceptive Jaquard, this glowed a very faint blue.

Petrone stepped forward. "We need a target, General."

"A target?" Jaquard's doubt was plain to see. "For that thing?" When neither junior officer responded, he shrugged and turned, gesturing absently at a sturdy wooden chair resting near the far wall. He was running out of patience for what increasingly appeared to be an elaborate farce. If it was not more, not a good deal more, the ranks of the defenders of Tesselar would be reduced by two officers.

"Defend the chair," Petrone requested.

This really had gone far enough, Jaquard felt. But having already sat through the first two acts of the play, he decided he might as well stay for the conclusion. Drawing the potent service wand from his own holster, he aimed it at the inoffensive chair. The wand was gilded and embedded with filigreed electrum, a gift from an admiring council upon his last promo-tion. For all its embellishment, in the hands of a twelfth-degree adept like himself it was frighteningly powerful.

"*Horfon descrine immutablius!*" he rumbled authoritatively.

A thin shaft of purple light lanced from the tip of the wand to strike the chair, which was immediately enveloped in a globe of amethyst radi-ance. The glowing sphere was bright and perfect and impenetrable. It would take an equal force, precisely focused and restricted, to so much as dimple it. The Horfon was the strongest singular defensive spell Jaquard knew. On the city wall, it had once saved him from an enemy slashing corkscrew summons that had felled half a dozen brave but lesser soldiers around him and left a foot-deep hole in the stone surface itself.

Petrone nodded at the lieutenant and stepped back. "Show him, Kemal."

Holding it in both hands, the lieutenant raised the tube and pointed the narrow end at the distant chair. Jaquard waited for the murmur of an incantation. It did not come. Instead, the young man pulled back on a small piece of metal that protruded from the underside of the tube. Another piece of metal on the top flicked downward, very fast. Powder ignited. Ignited, a stunned Jaquard observed, without so much as a whisper from either junior officer. There was a brief, bright flash of light and smoke. It was followed by a tremendous bang that echoed off the stone walls of the chamber. This despite the lieutenant not having voiced so much as a hint of a thunder spell.

It all happened so fast. The light and the smoke were followed by the lieutenant taking a forced step to the rear as the end of the tube kicked up and backward. That was the sum of it. As theater, it was certainly impressive. But as a device beyond its ability to startle it appeared to have no practical use. Recovering his poise, Jaquard said as much.

Petrone was decidedly smiling now. Jaquard did not like it when others got the joke and he did not. "Is that all it does?" he muttered uncertainly. Petrone gestured. "Let us check the chair, General."

Dubiously, Jaquard followed the captain across the room. The purple sphere of the Horfon still surrounded it, refulgent and intense as ever. It took the general a moment before the impossibility of what he was seeing registered fully on his brain.

In the back of the heavy wooden chair was a hole big enough to push a finger through. Leaning close, he saw that the edges of the hole were ragged and torn as if by a powerful piercing curse. Beyond, the stone wall was scored where the metal ball had struck it after passing completely through the chair. The Horfon continued to hover in place, apparently intact. It had been penetrated as if it consisted of nothing but air and words.

Petrone was clearly enjoying his superior's reaction. "Imagine, General Jaquard, if this chair was the chest of a Misarian soldier."

"It's not possible." Straightening, a disbelieving Jaquard turned to look first at the captain, then at the lieutenant. "This contravenes every known law of nature!"

"Did I not say it represents a new way of looking at the world?" Petrone murmured.

Striding over to confront the lieutenant, Jaquard extended both hands and asked, as deferentially as any supplicant before a spelling physician, "May I?"

His countenance a mixture of pride and bashfulness, Kemal handed over the stun. It was heavier than Jaquard expected, but not unbearably so. He studied it carefully.

"How does it work?" he asked without taking his eyes off the device.

The lieutenant proceeded to explain. "The powder is a special mixture of my own devising. Its components are quite commonly found in the ground and require little in the way of preparation. Nothing like a hammerspell or levitation necromancing." Leaning forward, he pointed. "When this small held stone and this piece of metal come together, the powder is ignited and ..."

"Just a minute." Jaquard looked up. "Let me make sure I am understanding this. The powder is ignited by bringing together a rock and a piece of metal? No incantation of any kind is involved? Not even the most basic fire spell?"

His shyness compelling him to glance downward, Kemal replied. "That's correct, sir."

A disbelieving Jaquard turned to Petrone. "The fire spell was perhaps the first basic incantation discovered by our primitive ancestors. Yet this device creates fire by bringing together pieces of wholly inert rock and metal? How can this be?"

Proud but honest, the captain replied straightforwardly. "I have no idea, sir. When I first saw a demonstration of the process, I was as incredulous as yourself."

"Fire without a fire incantation. Such a thing has never been imagined." Jaquard looked up sharply. "If it is not born of conjuration, it cannot be countered by conjuration."

"That is my way of thinking also, General." The lieutenant spoke solemnly.

Turning, Jaquard gestured in the direction of the shattered chair. "What propels the ball with such force?"

Letting the general continue to hold the stun, the lieutenant proceeded to explain. "The entire force of the sudden fire is trapped within the tube. This force drives the ball forward and with great velocity out the only opening. In the absence of a directional spell, the length and straightness of the tube alone decide its course."

"Astounding." A glint appeared in the general's eyes. "Can you make more than one of these?"

The lieutenant glanced at the captain, who smiled back. "I don't see why not, sir," the younger man declared. "With the help of skilled hands, the process of manufacture could be greatly accelerated."

"The powder," Jaquard pressed on. "Where does it come from?"

"That's the interesting thing, sir. Ample supplies of most ingredients are present within the grounds of the city itself. The only other critical component is readily available on at least two of the islands in the inner harbor." He hesitated, added, "It is the residue of the seabirds that nest there."

"The residue of ..." Now it was the general's turn to break out into a wide grin. "Are you telling me that one of the vital components of this deadly magic you have devised is bird shit?"

"It's not magic, sir," Petrone corrected him tactfully. "It's something else. We don't have a name for it yet." He looked at his protégé and smiled. "That is, Lieutenant Kemal does not have a name for it yet."

All trace of Jaquard's lethargy had vanished. He was once more a determined, fervent soldier of the Kingdom, eager to do battle. And what a battle it was going to be, he mused, envisioning the effect on the confident Misarians when ball after ball of despised and debased, ordinary unenchanted lead smashed through their strongest incantations to deal death and injury. They would not understand what was happening to them. Not understanding, they would panic, turn, and flee, to be driven from the Kingdom's shores forever.

Handing the unnatural weapon back to its maker, he reached down to the table to pick up one of the metal balls that had spilled from the cloth bag. Holding it up to a glowbulb, which drifted closer at his beckoning, he rolled the metal sphere back and forth between powerful thumb and weathered forefinger.

"This killing sphere, this innocent inert bit of meager lead: what do you call it? A stun-ball?"

"Well," Lieutenant Kemal murmured, "when I first got everything to work, the force of its strike reminded me of a charging bull. So I thought to call it a bull. But it's so much smaller than a bull I felt it necessary to add a diminutive. I call it a bullette."

"'Bullette.' And not a spell to be sensed anywhere about it. The Misarian misanthropes won't know what hit them. Their sorceral strategists will strive to emplace thaumaturgic defenses only to find themselves devastated by ordinary lead. Ordinary lead and," he added with an unmistakable hint of glee, "bird shit!" Putting down the innocent-seeming sphere, he turned back to the two waiting officers.

"Whatever you need, requisition it from stores and supplies. I'll sign the necessary orders. Work as fast as you can." He looked sharply at the lieutenant. "How quickly can you produce these stuns and bullettes?"

"It will take some time, sir," the lieutenant told him. "To fashion this one, by myself, required several years."

Jaquard's initial enthusiasm faded. "We don't have several years, Lieutenant."

"I know, sir. The enemy must be kept at bay while we make a start with the necessary manufacture. Realizing this, I set my mind to devise possible means by which we may delay and even drive them, at least temporarily, away."

"Another miracle," Jaquard muttered. He raised a hand. "Excuse me, gentlemen. Another way of thinking." He gazed hard at the lieutenant. "What did you have in mind, *Captain* Kemal?"

The lieutenant took the instant promotion in stride. "I'll need," he told his expectant commanding officer evenly, "a gryphon. And some men to help me collect more ingredients. A *lot* more ingredients. And several metal cylinders of the kind that are commonly used to store fresh milk."

In spite of what he had just witnessed, the general could not keep from repeating, "*Milk* containers?"

The new captain stared back at him. Suddenly, he did not look so young. "I'm going to try and make something a little bigger than a stun."

Several days later Jaquard and his senior staff were watching from the highest tower of the city walls as the lieutenant and his twin escort sped toward the blockading Misarian fleet. Major Petrone was present as well. The appearance of a squadron of gryphons heading toward them would have sparked an immediate response from the enemy, in force. A triplet of gryphons, without any escorting pixies or other military aerial manifestations, was presumed to consist of scouts who would stay high and not attempt to cast any spells. Any surprise incantations launched from altitude would, in any case, easily be countered by the fleet's alert defenses. Save for the Misarians half-heartedly conjuring a few flaming salamanders in their general direction, the high-flying trio from the besieged city was ignored. In any event, the sortie soared too high for the keening, combusting salamanders to reach. Failing to make contact with any targets they tumbled backward to land in the sea. There they promptly flamed out, hissing softly.

A personal magnifying spell hovering in front of him, General Jaquard watched as the three gryphons tilted their wings and banked sharply to the right. Riding wand on the middle gryphon, behind its pilot, Captain Kemal could be seen to lean out of his harness and drop something. It was a fairly large object and shaped like a teardrop. Observing this, Colonel Aspareal theorized aloud that it might be a crying spell designed to put out of action the sailors on one of the blockading ships, though what such a temporarily incapacitating incantation could hope to accomplish in the long run the good colonel could not imagine.

The gryphons banked sharply away. The teardrop shape struck not a ship but the dozing, finned serpent to which it was harnessed. There was a tremendous explosion. Jaquard found the startled cries of his experienced senior staff most gratifying, though he was hard-pressed, even though he had some idea of what was coming, to hold back his own astonishment.

When the smoke cleared, both ship and serpent were as before—except that the serpent was now missing its great, fanged, seaweed-fringed head. As the massive, serpentine, decapitated body sank beneath the waves, there was panic among the sailors on the ship. Deprived of its motive force, the vessel found itself suddenly at the mercy of the currents that ran outside the entrance to the harbor. It promptly slammed into the blockading vessel next to it before those aboard could rouse their own harnessed serpent to pull it out of the way.

A second teardrop fell from the hand of the middle gryphon's rider. This time its target was one of the largest ships in the blockading fleet. To their credit, the vessel's defenders were ready. A golden cloud appeared above the ship, passionate and beautiful. No gryphon, no dragon, no fire spell could penetrate it. Beneath, the defenders threw up a curtain of dismay designed to shunt any incoming enchantment harmlessly off to one side.

The heavy teardrop shape went right through the center of the golden cloud as if it was no more than a cloud, ignored the curtain of dismay as though it represented nothing more than the distraught thoughts of the officers who had commanded it forth, and struck the ship. A second explosion ripped through the air. By now it seemed as if half the besieged population of Tesselar had gathered atop the harbor walls to gesticulate and jabber excitedly. Some of them were jumping up and down and thrusting hands and fists in the air. A hole well and truly spelled (no, not spelled, Jaquard had to remind himself) in its hull, the Misarian ship began to sink rapidly. Distraught sailors could be seen leaping off its deck and sides. Desperate officers tried to repair the hole by declaiming several patching incantations. Because the perforation had not been caused by a spell, their efforts proved futile.

A sea-based squadron of gryphons was already launching from the Misarian flagship, but by now Captain Kemal and his triumphant escort were winging back to the city. Soon they would be safely within its outer defensive spells. Observing their approach, Jaquard realized that not only was it going to be possible to defend Tesselar, today represented a significant shift in the balance of power. The Kingdom would be saved. The equation had been changed. Thanks to the discoveries of a persistent, different-thinking junior lieutenant, warfare would never be the same again. *Nothing* would ever be the same again. If the powers-that-be so desired it, the Kingdom of Brevantis would become a force the likes of which the world had never seen. Or would at least until other lands and kingdoms independently made the same discoveries as the resourceful Captain Kemal. A way of doing things that was other-than-magic had been revealed. Undoubtedly, it would be exploited in ways a simple career soldier like himself could not foresee.

Though this would allow the salvation of his city and his country, General Jaquard was surprised to discover that his feelings about it were, at best, mixed.

8   OVERCAST

*O*ver the decades we've had a lot of pets. Cats, dogs, one Columbian red-tailed boa. All were rescued animals. Most were mellow to the point of somnolence. The boa loved, in its own strange, alien, reptilian way, children. You could put six-foot Sam on a one-year-old and it would slither slowly around the small body, delighting both him and the child. In the ten years I had Sam he never once bit anyone or tried to bite me, even when during a uniquely snakey illness I had to give him weekly subcutaneous fluids with a rather sizable hypodermic needle.

The same was true of the cats, who would either immediately take to visitors or run and hide: the antithesis of belligerence. Most of the dogs responded the same as the cats, often with attendant good-natured slobber, hopeful whining, and the presentation of toys for tossing.

Yet there was always one dog, just one, that was overly protective, and we would have to watch him around strangers, be they relative, friend, or workman. I'm sure those dogs felt they were just doing their job, being jealous and acting defensive. It sometimes made for some awkward moments.

But at least we always knew that the dog would react like a dog.

Eric had always enjoyed lying on his back outside and looking up at the clouds.

Though he had been doing it for thirty years, Sunday was the first time one looked back at him.

Or maybe he was just anthropomorphizing. That was, after all, one of the joys of cloud watching. Imagining the bunch of fluff off in the western sky looked like his twelfth-grade science teacher, Mr. Atkins. In his mind the milky swirl of cirrus directly overhead could easily be transmogrified into a distant memory of his beloved Aunt Grace. Those spotty strati off to the north were dead ringers for the lines of troops with whom he had marched in Iraq. But until now not a one of them—not Mr. Atkins, not Aunt Grace, not his buddies in the corps, had looked back at him.

Furthermore, it seemed to him as if it was coming closer.

Well, why not, he thought? As easy to experience two hallucinations as one. It was a small cumulus, not much bigger than his compact four-door and almost as faded. As it descended, he could not escape the feeling that it was looking at him. It had no eyes, of course. Not even Eric, with his expansive imagination, could transform puffs of vapor into eyes.

It halted a little more than an arm's length above him. Tugged by the wind, bits and pieces would be pulled away, reminding him of how as a child he used to tear pieces of cotton candy off the main mass and pop them in his mouth. Yet the cloud did not shrink in size. Renewing itself by gathering moisture from the air, he supposed. It was much too small to retain its shape. It was much too close to the ground. It was much too close to him. Alone on the forested hillside above Puget Sound, he sat up. The cloud retreated a few feet and continued to regard him.

This, Eric decided firmly, *was ridiculous.* He had a vivid imagination, but he was not crazy. He did not drink and did not ingest mind-altering substances. Whatever the source of the phenomenon, he knew he could simply walk away from it. Rising, he proceeded to do so.

The cloud followed.

It followed him down the slope, which was absurd. It followed him through the trees, which was impossible. It followed him all the way to the parking lot at the end of the trailhead. He half expected the persistent illusion to follow him into his car. Thankfully, it did not.

Feeling better, he headed home. Halfway back to Olympia it began to rain, heavily. Not an unusual occurrence in western Washington. Except— while it was raining all around him, puddling up against curbs and filling parking lots with temporary ponds, not a drop of moisture struck his car. He changed lanes, accelerated, slowed almost to stop. Nothing he did made any difference. Stopped at a red light, he stuck his head out the window with an eye toward scanning the sky. He found he could see it everywhere except overhead.

A thick mass of heavy and very localized cumulus hovered directly above his vehicle.

When the light changed to green, he accelerated gradually. Repeated glances outside showed that the cloud continued to keep pace, shielding his car from the storm. Aware that he was now gripping the wheel so tightly that his knuckles were beginning to cramp, he forced himself to consider the possibilities. Since not a one of them made any sense whatsoever, he decided he might as well go with the atmospheric flow, as it were. He had done so all his life, and while he might never be rich or famous, he could boast of low blood pressure and a general air of peace and contentment that escaped the high-tech hordes who had made an anthill out of the east side of the Sound.

I have acquired a cloud. So be it. He smiled to himself, wondering if it was the sort of smile that might cause others to edge carefully away from him should they encounter him on the street. He checked it in the rearview mirror. It was a perfectly normal smile, not crooked or twisted or otherwise reflective of mental derangement in any way.

His house was small but set outside town on a couple of acres of forested land. His nearest neighbor had considerably more land and raised horses. Eric preferred to raise Cain, but only on weekends and with close friends. He wondered how they might react to his new companion, assuming it stayed around. He opened the front door and entered. The cloud followed him right into the house.

Sitting down on the worn but welcoming old couch in the less than immaculate den, he flipped on the TV, watched three minutes of news, then turned the set off. He was not used to having a cloud in the room with him and it was proving hard to ignore.

"What am I going to do with you?" he wondered aloud. The cloud did not respond verbally. Instead, it drifted from one side of the den to the other, changing from puffy cumulus to leaner cumulostratus, and settled itself quietly into a corner. From time to time it would emit a puff of odorless wind in his direction.

He could do worse, he supposed. Ever since Orton, the street mongrel he had rescued, had died last year, he had gone petless. Could one pet a cloud? Rising from the couch, he walked over to it and extended a hand. It flinched slightly, reverting to full cumulus, but did not try to flee or evaporate.

"Steady," he heard himself murmuring, "easy there." He was very glad there was no one around to see what he was doing. His hand touched the cloud and slipped partway into it. Coolness and damp caressed his fingers. He withdrew them. When he did so, the cloud moved closer. After a couple of minutes of restrained human-atmospheric interaction, it turned cirrus, zipped several times around the room, and finally gathered itself as cumulus again into a tight, dense ball of cloud-stuff in front of the window that looked out onto the back of the property.

"I guess I'm going to have to let you stay," Eric murmured thoughtfully. In response, the cloud bobbed up and down in what might have been an indication of assent, or simply a momentary fluctuation in internal air pressure caused by the building's central heat coming on. "Guess I'll call you Aerol." He chuckled to himself. "Aerol Flynn."

The name didn't stick. For whatever reason, he soon came to believe that the cloud was by nature more feminine than male. This determination constituting only one more foolishness in a rapidly growing list of meteorological absurdities, he saw no problem in changing the cloud's name from Aerol to Aeriel. Certainly the cloud did not object.

While it only whispered to him via the occasional breeze and did not purr like a cat or bark like a dog, there were undeniable advantages to having a cloud as a companion. He did not have to walk it. When it had to go, it let him know by bumping repeatedly up against the back door. And when it relieved itself, which was no more than once or twice every several days, the hollyhocks and wildflowers in the yard were grateful beneficiaries.

At night it snuggled itself into the air above the master bedroom bathtub, though not before brushing past him to gently stroke his face. These repeated caresses imparted to his skin a healthy hydrological glow that others could not fail to notice. Female coworkers stopped him in the halls at work to ask what kind of moisturizer he was using. He could only reply that it was a natural substance he concocted himself, and alas, in quantities too miniscule to share.

On weekends and days off he would sit outside in the back yard, reading and soaking up the sunshine, a tiny bit of Mt. Rainier visible in the distance. If the sun became too harsh, the cloud would interpose itself between him and the sky. On the camping trips and long solo hikes in the Olympics that he so enjoyed, he no longer worried about finding a place to bathe. He would strip, stand wherever the view was satisfying, and Aeriel would run him through a personalized sprinkle, douse, and rinse cycle as required.

In return, the cloud asked little. A place to condense at night, occasional trips to a lake or the Sound to graze on moisture, sometimes play behind the house during which he would attempt to squirt her with a hose while she dodged or attenuated. She was always waiting for him when he came home at night. Dinner was usually pasta or fish for him, always a bucket of spring water for her. When it came time to do the dishes, he would soap them up and stick them, one at a time, into her. When he withdrew his hand and the glass or pot or dish, it was invariably sparkling clean. All he had to do was dry. Then she would settle down in the air behind him as he read or watched TV. Sometimes he read to her, and she would express her feelings with breaths of fresh air that were either warm or cold, depending on how she felt about the subject matter at hand.

He became a more than casual viewer of the Weather Channel. She loved it, hovering close at his shoulder as reports were filed and charts displayed, only occasionally whipping away to hide in the bedroom if a report of a hurricane or tornado came on the screen. Eric was content. The cloud was content. He met a girl.

He brought her home.

Jessica was short and vivacious, with bobbed black hair and obsidian eyes and a personality that was wonderfully unimpeded by convention. They met at work, then after work, then after after work and eventually on into the early mornings. Ideas were exchanged, notions were swapped, and before long it was mutually agreed that they were more than a little agreeable. He visited her apartment. She wanted to see his house. He wanted her to see his house, except ...

"I have a pet," he told her uneasily as they headed out of town on an overcast Saturday evening.

She laughed and pushed playfully at his shoulder. "Why do you think that would be a problem, Eric?"

Holding the wheel with both hands, he looked across at her. "You don't have any pets."

"No, but I feed half the stray cats in my neighborhood, and the occasional dog, and you always see seed in the birdfeeder outside my window."

He stared at the road ahead. The distance between her place and his kept getting shorter, and there was nothing he could do about it. "Mine's not a cat or a dog. Or a bird. Or a giant tortoise, or a lemur. It's not like any pet you've ever seen or heard of."

"Oh, come on, Eric!" She was shaking her head now, but affectionately.

"What is it, tell me. A lion? Do you have a lion? A poisonous snake? Is it something that's likely to bite me, or claw me?"

"No, no." He turned off the highway and down the street that meandered unavoidably toward his property. The forest that dominated the landscape seemed to close in around him. "It doesn't have any teeth, or any claws."

"I know," she declared excitedly, clapping her hands together, "it's a parrot! You've got a big, foul-tempered, dirty old parrot, or maybe a macaw, and you're afraid it won't like me and it's going to beak me to death."

He looked over at her. He had to smile. "Her name is Aeriel. At least, I've always thought of her as a 'her.'"

She frowned at him. "You mean you have a pet and you don't know what sex it is?"

"It's not easy to sex," he argued. When she started to protest, he raised a hand. "When you meet her, you'll see what I mean."

"Okay." Grinning, she sat back in the passenger seat. "Now you've got me really curious!"

The sun, insofar as its location could be determined on a typical northwest Washington day in late fall, was setting when they reached the house. Instead of pulling into the garage, Eric parked the car in the driveway. Outside, the air was cool and quiet.

"Now don't be shocked," he warned her as they walked up the paving stones he had set by hand. "Whatever you're anticipating, Aeriel's not going to be what you expect."

"I'm ready for anything." Taking his arm in hers, she snuggled close and batted goo-goo eyes at him. "My big bwave software progwammer will pwotect me." DeFudding her voice, she asked, "Is there a chance this mystery companion of yours might, um, leap into my arms?"

"Unlikely." He slipped the key into the front door lock. "But if she does, I guarantee she won't knock you over."

Sometimes the cloud was waiting for him in the hallway. Other times it waited elsewhere, giving him time to unburden himself of laptop, groceries, and any other baggage before greeting him. This evening it was waiting in the kitchen.

"Aeriel?" Tentatively, Eric entered the den. "Aeriel, we have company."

The cloud was hovering in the kitchen, above the stove. He often left it on for her. She loved to loiter in the column of warm, rising air. It was one of her favorite places.

As the cloud drifted out of the kitchen and into the den, Jessica's beautiful black eyes got bigger than marbles. "Eric, what ...?"

He took a deep breath. "Jessica, meet Aeriel. Aeriel, this is Jessica—my fiancée."

Cloud and woman regarded one another. Jessica started to say something, stammered, turned to look sharply at Eric, returned her gaze to the drifting cloud. As she did so, the cloud began to change.

Normally a pleasant, puffy cumulus shading to a relaxed altostratus, Aeriel was undergoing a metamorphosis that was as ominous as it was swift. She began to swell and expand, puffing herself up mightily, spreading upwards and outwards until she filled half the den and her roiling crest and splintering edges pushed threateningly against the walls and ceiling. She grew dark, darker than Eric had ever seen her before. She was cumulonimbus gray, then nimbus charcoal, then—she was black, black, a glowing, rumbling anvil-head.

She moved toward the couple.

Jessica took a step backward, and fell down. Mesmerized by the turbulent, roaring thunderstorm that now dominated the room, she started edging backward on her backside, pushing against the floor with her hands and feet. An anxious Eric hurried to position himself between his fiancée and the glowering cloud. Within the den, a wind was rising.

"Aeriel, you don't understand! There's no reason to be angry. This is the way people are, this is the way they're meant to be. It doesn't mean that you and I ..."

A sudden blast of wind, cold and wet, sent him staggering to his left. He slammed up against the wall, dimpling the plaster, and fought for balance. The howling wind held him pinned there. From deep inside the cloud, lightning had begun to flash and crackle. A furious rain filled the room, soaking furniture and the carpet. Jessica tried to rise, to run, but the wind knocked her legs out from under her.

"Aeriel!" Eric was shouting, "listen to me! Everything can be ...!"

Lightning lanced. It wasn't a very large bolt, but it was bright and intense enough to momentarily blind him. The smell of ozone filled the room. When he could see again, Jessica was no longer backing up. She was lying flat on the floor, eyes shut, curled up in a half-fetal position. An ugly black scar streaked her chest just below the right shoulder blade. Wisps of smoke were rising from the ragged slit that had appeared in her shirt.

Battling his way forward through the wind, Eric fell to his knees beside her. When he put a hand beneath her back and raised her up, her head hung free and loose. The moisture that welled up in his eyes was entirely self-generated. Today was supposed to have been a happy day, a joyous day. Whirling, he turned his furious gaze on the hovering, rumbling, ferocious thundercloud.

"Look what you—look what you ..." He swallowed hard, clenched his teeth. "Get out! Get out of my house, get out of my life! I don't want you here anymore! Do you hear me? I don't want to see you ever, *ever* again!"

For an instant the cloud was illuminated by so much internal lightning that its mere presence shorted out both the somnolent TV and the refrigerator in the kitchen. Eric held the limp form of Jessica tightly to him and closed his eyes. For a split second, the smell of ozone was in the air once again. There was a flash of light as bright as the sun and thunder shook the room, shaking books from their shelves and loosening plaster from the ceiling. A violent blast of hurricane-force wind rattled the house and blew out the picture window that dominated the back of the den.

Trailing thunderstorm-force winds in its wake like the cry of some long-extinct animal, the cloud swept out through the shattered window and was gone.

A trembling Eric crouched on the floor, still holding Jessica in his arms. It was the smoke that finally roused him. The last bolt of lightning had passed over their heads and set his old easy chair on fire. Letting Jessica down easy he stumbled into the kitchen, dragged out the fire extinguisher he kept stored in the cabinet beside the dishwasher, and returned to snuff out the flames before they could get a purchase on another piece of furniture or part of the house. By the time he was certain the fire was out, Jessica had begun to moan. It was the most wonderful sound he had heard in his life.

When the paramedics arrived, a dazed Eric managed to invent a disjointed but credible story about an arc springing unexpectedly from the TV to catch the chair on fire. The fact that the den and kitchen were soaking wet he explained by saying that the fire had caused the house's automatic sprinkler system to come on. Preoccupied as they were with the stunned but still alive Jessica, neither of the paramedics took the time to check the system to see if it actually had been activated.

Jessica recovered. When necessary, makeup covered the thin, jagged scar that now ran down the right side of her chest. She would not see him or speak to him for a long time. Then one day there came a phone call— hesitant, conciliatory if not exactly inviting. They met. Conversation resumed, then meetings. A love that had never entirely been blasted away by the lightning in Eric's den was rekindled, though when speaking of it both of them were careful not to employ any metaphors that involved mention of fire.

Gradually, the memory faded until the reality that it had once been passed into the realm of dream. They got along too well to place their personal lives in stasis at the expense of a nightmare. Marriage brought closure, success at work brought peace, and in the manner of things, time brought first a boy, then a girl. Eric had to enlarge the house.

Years passed. The joy of living in a beautiful part of the world brought rewards that could not be counted in dollars. The Sound remained the Sound; a uniquely beautiful part of the planet. Rainier continued to brood over its domain and maintain its long, peaceful sleep. The Olympic Range still thrust snow-streaked spires into oceans of white cloud and cerulean blue.

They were on a family hike in those mountains one day when, slowly but unmistakably, one of the many clouds showed signs of descending.

"The car." A grim-faced Eric stood his ground, facing the lowering mass of bulging whiteness. "Get the kids to the car." He knew how hopeless the suggestion was even as he said it. The car was miles away, downslope at the head of the trail. Eyes wider than they had been in many years, Jessica drew Andrew and Cissy to her.

The children were not frightened: they were fascinated. Cissy raised a hand and pointed. "Daddy, mommy, look! The cloud is coming to say hello!"

"Wow," was all the older Andrew could think to say. "I didn't know clouds could drop down like that."

Only certain clouds, an increasingly tense Eric knew. Only one cloud.

As it came steadily nearer, he took care to keep himself positioned between the descending cumulus and his family. "Get back into the trees, Jessica. Take the kids into the forest." It was a good quarter-mile sprint off the ridgeline trail to the nearest firs and spruces, but it was the only chance they had. If he could keep himself between the cloud and them ...

The cloud was almost on him now. Behind him, Jessica and the children had hesitated, had failed to make a run for it when they'd had the time. Now it was too late. A finger of cloud, a cold front in miniature, extended itself toward him. From within its depths came a first faint rumbling. The cloud touched him. Caressed him.

No words were spoken. No words had ever been spoken between

them. Like the tentacles of some ghostly cephalopod, wreaths of soft cloud wrapped themselves around him, stroking his hair, his face, his upper body. Unaware of the antecedents, the children looked on in fascination as their mother held them close. Then it rose to drift over and past him, heading for his family.

"Eric ..." Jessica began, unable to suppress the quaver in her voice.

"Mom, you're hurting me." Her arm was tight, tight, across Andrew's neck.

Eric started to move to intercept the cloud. What could he do if he got in its way? You couldn't fight air. But there had been something about the way it had touched him, caressed him. A familiar touch, from many years gone by. He was anthropomorphizing again, he knew. But unlike the first time, history gave him reason to do so without questioning his sanity.

"Jessica, relax. I think ..." He gazed at the slowly drifting cloud mass, "I think it's going to be okay."

As it had when facing him, fingers of cloud emerged from the main mass. Reached out toward Jessica, and touched. Touched and stroked. Eric relaxed, then he smiled. Time, he reflected, heals. Changes things.

Tentative at first, Jessica reached out too, inserting a hand into part of the cloud. It drew back, then paused, finally returning to envelop her up to the shoulder. The shoulder with the scar. She smiled.

"It tickles," his wife told him. "*She* tickles." Having been released from their mother's grasp, her children were laughing and giggling, jumping up and down as they, too, tried to touch the cloud.

It was all right now, Eric knew. Even the weather changes with time. Advancing, he put an arm around Jessica. The cloud did not object. Instead, it ascended slightly. As they moved off, resuming their hike and continuing on down the trail, the cloud moved with them, flattening out and spreading sideways to shield them from the glare of the midday sun.

Andrew and Cissy followed in their parents' wake. Occasionally they would pause to inspect this flower or that bug, sometimes smiling, sometimes fussing, occasionally pushing gently at one another.

Above each of them, a very small but bright cloud paced their progress.

9 THE ECCENTRIC

I haven't been to the exact location described in this story, but I've spent time in countries and villages very much like it. One responds differently to such locales the moment the sun goes down. During the day these small, isolated, mountain European villages are bright and cheery, with flowers blooming in every window box and people sweeping the often cobblestoned streets to keep them immaculately clean. The fountains always flow, there are usually birds singing, and cats doze in the sun atop high stone walls.

It's amazing how these bucolic scenes can change with the fall of night. The flowers shrink back in on themselves, slinking instead of sleeping the town cats morph into Halloween caricatures, and heavy wooden shutters close off each and every window with the finality of a bank vault, shutting out anything and everything that might be wandering the streets. Including innocent and often bewildered tourists.

Fortunately, there's usually some good soul out and about to take pity on the wandering visitor and rescue them from the looming dark....

Karen Roper had been making the rounds in Sighisoara for over a week without encountering a single soul who could introduce her to a werewolf. The generally accepted wisdom that there were no such things as werewolves had not dissuaded her. As a freelance writer who was relentless in her pursuit of the eerie, the bizarre, and the outré, she refused to be discouraged where so many who had come before her had given up. Aided and abetted by her good looks, persistence and determination had combined with a competency at writing to deliver a good living. The opportunity to travel to distant off-the-beaten-path destinations such as Sighisoara was an added bonus.

Unfortunately, her rambling visit to exotic Romania was turning out to be something of a bust. No novice nuns in remote villages had been considerate enough to endure fatal exorcisms while she was in the country, no mysterious forces had been deemed at work in what was still one of Europe's last primal countrysides. The best she had been able to come up with was a two-part article on some supposedly haunted Roman-era ruins. It had sold to one of her regular markets, but she had been forced by circumstance (and escalating hotel bills) to accept less than her going rate.

And then, on the verge of giving up and heading back to Bucharest to catch the next plane to Istanbul, she had met up with Bucazu.

He had responded over the phone to one of her numerous newspaper come-ons with whispers and insinuations. "I can show you werewolf, Miss Roper. There is place, special place. In mountain valley. Even authorities don't go there. They afraid since time of Ceasecu. Even before time of Ceasecu."

"It doesn't have to be a, um, 'real' werewolf," she'd told him. "At this point, I'll settle for a suitably ugly and really hairy peasant. A hunchback would be nice. With a third of the remaining real wolves in Europe being here in Romania I can, um, stretch the truth a little."

Either the man on the other end of the line had misunderstood, or else the sardonicism was completely lost on him despite his evident, if quaint, command of English.

"No, Miss Roper. Real werewolf. Like in old legends. But is dangerous."

Well, of course it was dangerous, she had smiled to herself. If it wasn't declared "dangerous," a presumably gullible visiting foreigner like herself was unlikely to take the bait. Still, it was something, which was better than the nothing she was finding in and around Sighisoara.

"Okay," she had told him. "I'll take you up on it." She would hazard a last try for material and, with luck, a saleable photo or two before departing for Istanbul in search of contemporary djinn.

Having spent time traveling by herself researching articles in places like Afghanistan and Laos, she was confident she could handle one Romanian huckster. To her surprise, when her guide showed up later that night, it was in a Mercedes. An old Mercedes, to be sure, but not some antique Communist-era rattletrap, either. Furthermore, Bucazu himself turned out to be a tall, willowy young man with the body of a slender Viking, an impenetrable thicket of black hair that must be the bane of any barber, and the manners of a young European gentleman instead of that of the thrash metal enthusiast a first glance might have suggested. He even opened the car door for her: the back door.

Clutching the bag containing her overnight gear and laptop under her left arm, she paused at the doorway. "I'm hiring you as a guide—not a chauffeur."

"*Va rog*—please forgive me." Shutting the rear door, he opened the front passenger-side door in its stead. "I thought you might feel safer—that is, be more comfortable, in the back."

She almost laughed. After having rattled through Kandahar in the company of three overly attentive AK-47 toting militiamen, she had no fear of being forcefully cuddled by one somewhat skinny young Romanian.

"It's kind of you to think of me like that, but I'm sure I'll be—comfortable—in the front seat." She tapped her bag. "I might want to take a picture of something."

"Not tonight." He started around toward the other side of the car. "We will arrive in Koska before daybreak. Maybe good picture tomorrow."

She slid in opposite him. Bucket seats and raised center console made his concern for her person seem even more superfluous. "When do I get to meet your werewolf?"

The Mercedes started up smoothly and pulled away from the hotel entrance. "Tomorrow night is the fullness of the moon. That is why we had to hurry and leave now, tonight. Tomorrow night you will see werewolves."

Though aware that his English was less than perfect, she still blinked. "You mean 'werewolf.'"

He looked over at her. For the first time, she was aware of the intensity of his gaze. "No, Miss Roper. 'Were*wolves*.' There are many in Koska. And I think other things of interest to you as well."

"Lots of hairy guys?" she quipped, unable to take him seriously in the slightest.

"You will see," he assured her as the heavy sedan accelerated out onto a main thoroughfare.

Oh well, she thought as she snuggled back into the thick, cushioning seat. Having spent most of her time in Bucharest and Sighisoara, it would be nice to see some more of the countryside before moving on to Turkey.

Determined to stay awake, she had no idea how long she had slept when the slowing of the car revived her. Automatically and surreptitiously, she checked everything of consequence. Her bag lay on the floor by her feet, apparently undisturbed. The same was true of her clothing. Her almost painfully earnest young escort was not looking in her direction when she awoke, his gaze still fixed firmly forward. She was impressed—and a little relieved.

The village of Koska was charming even at night. Multi-story wooden houses, some of them hundreds of years old, lined the cobblestone street down which they were proceeding. The Mercedes's suspension smoothed out the bumps. At this hour all the streetlights had been extinguished to save electricity, but the almost full moon allowed her to make out numerous architectural details and flourishes; everything from elaborately carved wooden lintels to the painted flowers and other traditional designs that decorated the houses. They passed a small market, a real bakery, and the local pharmacy before pulling up before an urbanized country inn. Even at four in the morning and visible only by moonlight, the outside looked like an outtake from Disney's *Pinocchio*. If the rooms were half as charming as the exterior, she was going to enjoy her brief stay here.

"I leave you now." Bucazu indicated the darkened entrance. "Just ring bell. I phone ahead and tell the innkeeper's family to be expecting an early arrival guest." He did not quite smile. "These are country folk, and they will be up soon with sun anyway, so do not feel you imposing by checking in at this hour."

She nodded, started to get out of the car, hesitated. "You're not coming?"

"Koska is my home. That is how I could promise you werewolf. But only on night of full moon. Tomorrow night." He took a deep breath. "Have to sleep now. I not nap on way from Sighisoara. Good driver," he finished proudly.

"No argument here," she complimented him. "You'll be wanting to sleep in, for sure."

"Da," he told her. "I will get good rest so that tomorrow night I will be

alert and ready to—to show you what you have come to see." He indicated her bag. "I hope you have plenty film in your camera."

"It's digital," she told him. "No film."

"Oh, of course. When it come to consumer electronics, I afraid I am bit behind the times." He offered an embarrassed smile. "Country boy."

Despite what he had told her about having notified the innkeeper of her arrival, he still waited in the car until the door opened in response to her ring. Polite *and* considerate, she mused thoughtfully. Not bad-looking, either. And he hadn't hit on her or tried anything while she had been dozing in the car. It might be fun to spend some time with him, she told herself. After interviewing and photographing the werewolf. No. She smiled to herself. Were*wolves*. Despite his promise she would be more than satisfied with just one reasonable approximation thereof.

The heavy wooden comforter-filled second-floor bed was more restful than those in any of the hotels where she had stayed the previous weeks. It was noon when she finally woke up. Downstairs, a hearty Eastern European lunch awaited her, served by the innkeeper's wife and pre-teen daughter. The girl in particular was a delight, a small solemn-faced whirlwind bedecked with golden curls, rosy cheeks, and deep blue eyes. Only the jeans and T-shirt, the latter alluding to a Hungarian rock band she'd never heard of, spoiled the Heidi-esque illusion.

She'd planned to take a stroll around the town, but the long drive the night before combined with the heavy midday meal and thoughts of the overstuffed bed to lure her back to the room. She read herself to sleep, awakening only in time for dinner.

Except there was no dinner. But Bucazu was waiting for her in the tiny lobby, sitting and perusing a magazine opposite the empty, gray stone fireplace. Of the kindly innkeeper and his family there was no sign.

"Full moon tonight." Bucazu's tone was grave. "Everyone in town must take certain precautions."

"Oh, of course." Camera and anticipation at the ready, Karen was eager and willing to go along with the gag. "What about precautions for us?"

"You will be safe with me," he assured her. She had to give him credit for maintaining the artifice. "As I have told you, I live here, so I am known to everyone. Those who be 'were' can recognize me even in their altered state. Otherwise it would be dangerous for me, too, to travel alone outside on such a night. Because you are with me, you too will be safe.

But stay close. Take all the pictures you want, but do not stray from my side."

If that was a pick-up line, she mused, it was for sure unlike any she had never encountered before.

"All right," she told him. "I'm ready."

"It not dark out, and moon is not up yet."

She shrugged, completely at ease. "I slept in. Now that I'm awake, I can always kill time with a little window shopping."

"There not much in the way of such things in Koska," he told her. "This town not on any of usual tourist routes. But we can walk if you like."

He was right. Those shops that might have contained interesting crafts or handmade knick-knacks were closed and shuttered tight for the night. Still, she enjoyed the stroll. Until the howling began.

It flat-out chilled her. She had walked past bodies that had been blown to bits by landmines or shredded by glass and shrapnel, had seen the bloated disfigured corpse of a Thai farmer killed by a king cobra, had listened to the wails of women whose children had been murdered in internecine fighting. But none of that, nothing she had seen or heard before, had raised the hackles on her neck like that rolling, rumbling, infinitely *disturbed* howling. It was for damn sure no mournful dog.

Until just then, she hadn't even realized she had hackles.

"Jesus!" she muttered.

"Not here," Bucazu responded enigmatically. "Not tonight. Stay close."

The ferociously throaty challenge grew louder as they made their way toward the town square. A relic of medieval times, it was dominated by an equestrian statue of some obscure local military hero surmounting a graven stone base featuring four tinkling spigots. The familiar sound of running water was unexpectedly reassuring. She swallowed hard.

"Over here," her escort told her, intense as ever. "This way."

Leading her to an arched doorway, he produced an iron key seemingly as old as the town itself. She could hear the tumblers clinking like marbles as he turned it in the lock's appropriate recess. Standing close but not trying anything, he leaned down and pointed toward the equestrian fountain. Over the distant line of ragged mountains a bilious moon was leering, casting its curdled luminance across the shadowed cobblestones of the square.

"Watch, wait, and keep quiet," he told her. This time, she ventured no clever quip in response. She was not sure she could have done so had she wished, so dry was her throat.

A shape shambled into the square, then another, and another. Some were huge, some merely outsize, others almost diminutive—but never dainty. A few wore clothes, or shards of same, while others were unclad. All were hirsute to the point of shaggy overkill. The fur of some was black, of some brown, and others were splotched or striped in more exotic patterns. They howled and moaned and kicked and scratched. Some fought ferociously, others chased one another around the square. One bounded to the top of the statue—a single clean, unbroken leap of some twenty vertical feet, she estimated—threw back its head, and bayed disdainfully at the still rising moon. No wonder, she thought as she stared, that the town of Koska prepared so carefully for nights on which there was a full moon.

They were *all* werewolves.

A town of werewolves. Real ones, not like cheaply faked Bigfoots or imitation Yetis. Directly in front of her, a pair was breeding. Their mating was rough, primordial, and very, very loud. No one noticed her and her escort, huddled in the deep sheltering darkness of the ancient doorway.

She looked up at her companion in sudden fear; the kind of fear she hadn't felt in years, if ever. "You—you live here, Bucazu, but you're not —you're not ...?"

"Not 'were'? Not one of *them*? No," he assured her solemnly. He never seemed to smile, she observed. Living here, she could now understand why. "My family has resided here long time, so the changelings, they tolerate me."

"Why in heaven's name don't you move away? Lord, it would only take one of them to change their mind one night and decide to rip you up for dinner!"

"We have agreement," he murmured firmly. "I think they find a non-changeling willing to live in their midst something of a novelty." He indicated her bag. "Your camera?"

Omigod—she had been so stunned by the feral, orgiastic sight that she had forgotten what she'd come for. Fumbling frantically at the bag, she whipped out the compact device, made sure the media card was seated, double-checked to make certain the flash was off, and began snapping away. A quick preliminary check of the LCD screen showed that this was no discouraging fantasy—each picture came out, though depending on the available moonlight some were of course sharper than others. What could she demand for the first indisputably authentic, unfaked photo of a genuine, real, honest-to-gypsy-legend werewolf? A million bucks? What could she ask for dozens of such photos? No more gallivanting around the globe in search of obscure, difficult-to-research stories. Not for this girl. After tonight she would be able to gallivant all she wished without having to work, and gallivant in high style.

Standing at her shoulder, Bucazu helpfully pointed out especially dramatic scenes: two female werewolves battling, a pack of youngsters snarling and scrapping as they tore apart a stray dog unfortunate enough to have wandered onto the square, two adolescents playing tag—by bounding from rooftop to rooftop, clearing impossible gaps and incredible distances with each leap.

Notes—she could make notes later. In the morning. No way was she going to be able to sleep. The realization made her turn to her escort; her wonderful, gracious, knowing escort who was going to make her rich. Despite her somewhat limited resources his tip, she decided, would have to be commensurate with the miracle he had wrought for her.

"What happens in the morning?"

"They all turn back, of course. Into normal Koska villagers. Until next full moon. Tomorrow day is all normal—except town doctor is usually very busy. Many cuts and scrapes and bitings to treat. But no disease. No rabies. The wereblood is very powerful. Vital. There is no sickness here, in Koska."

"This is fantastic, this is great!" she kept mumbling as she snapped shot after shot, pausing only intermittently to check her results on the camera's LCD.

It was when she was switching storage chips that she heard the snarl. It was much closer, much more—intimate—than the canid cacophony that continued to fill the square unabated. Looking up from the camera she saw an enormous wolf, its black fur tipped with silver, the largest she had seen all night. It was staring straight at her, freezing her where she stood, advancing on enormous paws. Its powerful claws click-clicked on the cobblestones.

"I thought you said," she whispered in abject terror, "I thought you said we would be safe."

His arm went around her shoulders. "Always a bully in any town," he muttered. "Always one who must show himself off. Or maybe he just hungry. Come!"

He half pulled, half pushed her inside, pulling the door shut behind them. An instant later something smashed into the door with tremendous force. Roper's ears rang from the concussion. The door buckled, albeit slightly. It sounded as if it had been hit by a runaway bus.

She continued to back away, only to bump into Bucazu. He did not appear overly concerned. "Do not to worry. Door is four-hundred-year-old oak bound with iron. Hinges are forged. Missile might break through, but not wolf."

Sure enough, after several minutes of frustrated howling and screaming, scratching and pounding, the horror on the other side of the doorway went away. From what she could hear through the thick, life-saving wood, the chorus of hell was still in full swing out on the square, however.

"More pictures?" her solicitous escort inquired politely.

Aware that she was shaking badly, she nonetheless nearly broke out laughing. "No. No thank you, Bucazu. I have more than enough. Considerably more than I expected to shoot tonight, if you must know." She steadied herself. "This is unbelievable! A whole village populated by werewolves! Real werewolves, not fakes made up to draw tourists. I can't believe it. Nobody will believe it—until the pictures are authenticated." She turned to face him. "Thank you, Bucazu, thank you! I'm a woman of my word, and you can believe me when I say that I'm going to make this night worth your while!"

"I know," he told her quietly.

"As soon as I can put together an accompanying article, and get the photos emailed and verified as non-fakes, I'll—" She broke off, frowning at him. "What do you mean, 'you know'?"

"I always thought bringing you here would be worth the time I would invest."

"Oh. Oh sure, of course. Anyway, as soon as ..." For the second time she broke off. "Bucazu, why are you looking at me—that way?" She tensed, but there was no hint of incipient canid transformation, no indication that her escort was were-anything. But there was also no denying the distinct gleam that had come into his eyes.

For the first time that night, he smiled. He smiled, and she sucked in her breath. She wanted to scream, but could not. No hair sprouted from his face, no fur thrust forth to dimple his neat, perfectly creased clothing. He was unchanged, except for the look that had come into his eyes and the unusually long canine teeth his smile had exposed. Long they were, and sharp, and pointed. At that moment it also struck her that he was not looking at her eyes, or even at her face, but at a location on her body slightly lower down. The camera with its precious and now meaningless pictures fell to the floor as the hand that had been holding it rose reflexively to her neck.

"You have no idea, my beautiful and vibrant Miss Roper," he told her sorrowfully as he came toward her, hands outstretched and teeth gleaming, "how *lonely* it is for me here."

10   DARK BLUE

Okay, another real estate story. Except I have been to this locale. To the exact place. It's in the oceanic version of the middle of nowhere. Pretty much where a certain renowned writer would sensibly have located it, if only he had been able to visit the region himself. Being something of a homebody, he never managed to do so. But he and I share an abiding fascination for the sea and what dwells therein.

Since he was never able to get to such a place, or any remotely (pun intended) like it, I thought I might try to do so for him, filling in the necessary gaps in unfathomable (hey, another pun!), unknown, eldritch, cyclopean, geographic lore on his behalf. I like to think he would have approved. Would perhaps even have responded with a knowing, sinister, smile....

The sea below the keel of the ocean-going ketch *Repera* was the bluest blue Chase Roentgern had ever seen. It was bluer than blue. Bluer than the clearest sky, bluer than all the lapis-lazuli in Afghanistan, bluer than sapphire or azurite or a studio track by Coltrane. Roentgern had spent considerable time on a number of boats on two oceans but he had never seen blue like this. He asked Captain Santos about it.

"There are no fish here, in this deep, deep water. No fish because no zooplankton. No zooplankton because no phytoplankton." Standing on the flying bridge with his long hair tucked under his cap and dark wrap-around shades shielding his eyes from the sun and wind, Santos nodded to port. "With no microscopic life in the water, no life of any kind, there nothing to scatter the sunshine. Everything get absorbed except the blue. The sun pour down unobstructed and just keep going, going, until it fade away to indigo-black."

Roentgern nodded his understanding as he raised the expensive binoculars that were hanging from the padded strap around his neck. They hadn't seen a thing since leaving Pitcairn behind. Only a few patrolling seabirds searching diligently for the fish Santos insisted were not there.

They had tried but had been unable to land at Pitcairn. The island's famous swells were too high for their single rigid inflatable to chance a dash for the concrete and rock breakwater that protected the tiny artificial harbor at Bounty Bay, and given the rough conditions the islanders were not inclined to risk one of their vital Moss aluminum longboats just to venture out and say hello to those on board a tramp ketch like the *Repera*.

As it had sailed on eastward out of sight of Pitcairn's towering green-clad peaks, Roentgern had reflected in passing that the original Bounty mutineers had indeed succeeded in isolating themselves on one of the least accessible islands in the entire South Pacific. Now the *Repera* was headed for a speck of land that was even more inaccessible than Pitcairn, and devoid even of the resilient descendants of rowdy mutineers and their dedicated vahines.

A more or less oval chunk of solid coralline limestone rising straight up out of the ocean from a depth of three and a half kilometers, Henderson Island lay another two hundred kilometers northeast of Pitcairn, which in turn was more than twice that distance from where he had met up with the *Repera* in the Gambier islands of southern French Polynesia. The nearest airstrip to Henderson was on Mangareva, more than six hundred kilometers away in the Gambiers. No aircraft could land on Pitcairn and it was too far to reach by chopper. The closest outpost of civilization to Henderson in the other direction was Easter Island, which lay so far over the dead-flat horizon that the inhabitants of Mangareva were next-door neighbors by comparison.

"Why on Earth would you want to go to a god-forsaken place like this Henderson?" his wealthy friends had asked him once he'd explained what and where it was. "Why not go to Maui, or the Bahamas? You say there's nothing on Henderson but birds, and you're not a birder."

That much was true. Chase Roentgern did not tally bird sightings.

Nor was he an especially avid scuba diver. What he did collect was money, and at that he was very good.

For more than two years he had been researching the history of ships that had gone missing in Henderson's vicinity. Ships that had been blown off course, or had become lost due to navigational error, or had simply foundered in storms. Vessels that disappeared in this part of the Pacific well and truly vanished. No ship that encountered serious trouble in the azure wasteland could expect help.

Since leaving Mangareva they had seen exactly one other vessel; a big container ship heading for Cape Horn. Most commercial traffic bound from the South Pacific for the Atlantic took the easier, much faster route north to the Panama Canal. As for fishing boats, there were no long-liners here, no purse seiners, because as Captain Santos had pointed out, there were no fish. There were no fish because there was nothing for them to eat. Concerning bottom trawlers—the bottom was three or four kilometers down and unknown. Too deep to trawl safely for too little potential reward for a big dragliner to take the risk.

When Henderson itself finally hove into view days later its appearance was something of an anticlimax. Roentgern was not disillusioned. The reality matched the few pictures he had been able to find of the place. Unlike Bora Bora or Rarotonga, Pacific islands that boasted dramatic central peaks and gleaming turquoise lagoons, Henderson was a makatea island. Several others were scattered around the Pacific; huge blocks of limestone and coral that had been uplifted and exposed to the air when the sea levels had fallen during the last ice age. Not only were they usually devoid of beaches, a visitor could not even walk very easily on a makatea. Rain eroded the limestone into razor-sharp, boot-slicing, flesh-shearing blades and pinnacles of solid rock.

As opposed to animals and humans, certain well-adapted birds and vegetation thrived in the otherwise hostile makatea environment. Shearwaters and noddys, petrels and four species of endemics made their home on Henderson. Its only regular human visitors were Pitcairners who came once or twice a year to collect valuable hardwood like miro for the carvings that constituted a substantial part of their income. Other than that, Henderson had been left to the birds, the crabs, a few lizards, and the ubiquitous Polynesian rat. Except for one rumored spring visible only on the single narrow beach at low tide there was not even any fresh water to be had. Not a good place, Roentgern reflected, on which to be marooned.

But then, he was not interested in spending time on Henderson, however wildly attractive the place might be to the rare visiting scientist.

It was a photograph that had finally brought him to this, one of the most isolated tropical islands on Earth. It was the same photograph that had led him to charter the *Repera* and its somewhat taciturn but capable crew. His cultivated friends in New York had been right about one thing: no one anywhere much wanted to go to Henderson. It had taken him months, a lot of searching on the net, and an extensive exchange of querulous emails before he found a captain with a ship willing to travel so far from the bounds of civilization, to waters where no help could be expected in the event of trouble, no passing ship could be hailed for assistance, and there was nothing to see and no one to visit.

Happily, in the course of their exchange of emails Salvatore Santos had not pressed his prospective employer for a trip rationale. All that had been necessary was to agree on a price.

Henderson slid past astern, its stark white thirty-meter high cliffs gleaming like chalk in the sun, its population of seabirds forming a flat, hazy gray cloud above the trees as they cherished the one bit of dry land for hundreds of kilometers in every direction. The island was still in view astern when Roentgern checked his GPS one more time, turned to the Captain, and declared with confidence, "This is the place."

Looking up from the wheel and his bridge instruments, the unshaven Portuguese-Tahitian squinted at his employer. "Here?" He waved a sun-cured hand at the surrounding sea, which obligingly had subsided almost to a flat calm. "You want to drop anchor *here?*"

Roentgern smirked. He knew something the Captain didn't know. If his two years of painstaking research was right, he knew something *nobody* else knew. With the possible exception of the bored astronaut on board the space shuttle who had taken the photograph that the energetic Roentgern had scanned in more detail than anyone at NOAA or NASA.

"Check your depth finder."

Santos had not bothered to look at that particular readout since leaving Pitcairn. The ocean out here was benthonic, and even this close to Henderson it dropped off sharply into the abyss. Under the circumstances, the captain showed remarkable aplomb as he checked the relevant monitor and reported.

"What do you know? There is an uneven but largely flat surface thirty meters directly below us. I am assuming it is a seamount. It is very small for such underwater features and at a depth that renders it harmless to passing ships, of which there are not any around here anyway. So it not surprising it is absent from the charts."

"It's not all that small." Having looked forward for so long to springing this knowledge on someone else, Roentgern found that he was enjoying himself immensely. "And it's not just a seamount."

Santos eyed him doubtfully. Out of the corner of an eye Roentgern could see several members of the half-dozen strong crew watching the two men from the deck. The captain finally smiled.

"Ah, I understand now. You are a crazy man. I knew that when you hired me and my boat to bring you all this way. But that didn't bother me. A man can be as crazy as he like, so long as his money is sane."

Kneeling, Roentgern opened the small watertight Pelican case that occupied a compartment on the bridge near his feet. It contained none of the expensive camera gear it was designed to coddle and protect. Instead, it was full of envelopes, flash drives, and a laptop computer. Selecting and unsealing one of the envelopes, he removed several glossy 8X10 prints and handed the top one to Santos.

"Have a look at this."

The captain examined the photo with fresh interest. "Henderson," he observed immediately. "Taken from space. View slightly from the south. Even with the clouds, you can't mistake the shape."

"Very good." Roentgern handed him the next picture.

Studying it, Santos frowned. "Henderson again, much closer view." He tapped the picture with a forefinger. "Here; the water is so clear, you can see a suggestion of the seamount we are over right now."

Roentgern repressed a knowing smirk as he passed over the third and last picture. "That last one was a blowup, multiple magnification. Here's a much better one, with the resolution computer and radar-enhanced and corrected for depth, shadow, atmospheric distortion, and other obscuring factors I needn't go into in detail."

Santos studied the picture. Looked at it for a long time. Then he handed it back to its owner. "I still think it is nothing but a seamount."

"Seamounts have broken crowns. Or they're conical in shape. Or capped with solidified lava, or they sport a sunken lagoon." He gestured with the photo. "This one is as flat on top as a Los Angeles parking lot. Except for the bumps. Bumps with very distinctive shapes."

A corner of the captain's mouth twitched slightly upward. "You think it is a parking lot?"

Roentgern had to laugh. "I'm not crazy, Salvatore, despite what you might think. Those 'bumps' are ships that have gone down here. At least four, maybe as many as ten. Maybe more than that, once we get down there. Two of the four are definitely pre-nineteenth century. You know what that means? Maybe treasure galleons that were sailing back to Spain from the Philippines. Trying to sneak around the Horn instead of sailing to Peru or Panama along routes that were haunted by English privateers like Drake. Before they could reach the Horn, they got lost or slammed into Henderson's rocks. Most went down to the depths. But a few"—and again he tapped the photo—"a few fetched up here. At a depth reachable with nothing more elaborate than conventional sport diving equipment." He stared hard as he slipped the pictures back into the envelope. "Put down the anchor."

Santos hesitated a moment longer. Then he shrugged. "It your money, Mr. Roentgern. You may be right. There may be a ship or two down there. But I no think there any treasure. And even if there is, anything we might find belong to the British government. Henderson is part of the Pitcairn British Overseas Territory."

"That's absolutely correct." With slow deliberation, Roentgern returned the envelope to the watertight case. "And you can see for yourself how well this part of that territory is policed. Should we find anything we'll declare it immediately when we return to Mangareva. I'm sure you will be the first to go out of your way to inform the British consul in Papeete about any discoveries we may make."

The captain pursed his lips. To Roentgern they almost seemed to be moving slowly in and out, in and out, in concert with the captain's thoughts. Finally Santos smiled; a broad, wide smile.

Roentgern nodded curtly. He had gambled on just such a reaction. As soon as he had met Santos, he knew it was not much of a gamble. "We understand each other, I think."

"Perfectly, Mr. Roentgern. I will tell Bartolomeo to start readying the scuba gear."

The water was not just clear: in the absence of microscopic pelagic life and located thousands of kilometers from the nearest source of pollutants, it was virtually transparent. As soon as he hit the water and started down, Roentgern felt as if he was diving in air. The only sound following his entry was the regularity of his respiration and the sporadic mutter of bubbles from the regulator. As for the questions that had brought him to this isolated corner of the planet, they were answered as soon as he entered the water.

Just by looking down and without the aid of any special equipment he could see the outlines of sunken ships resting atop the seamount thirty meters below. Not only could he see the ships, the water was so clear that he could identify each vessel's type, condition, approximate age, and a host of other informative factors. Twisting as he slowly descended fins first, he located Santos and gave him the thumbs-up sign. His hair drifting lazily behind him like black seaweed, the captain nodded and responded in kind.

Inclining his head and body downward, an excited Roentgern accelerated his descent.

Inner exploration of the various shipwrecks and the actual search for treasure and other valuables would take place on future dives, with additional equipment. A thirty-meter descent would require a proper surface interval before the next dive. No matter. Now that his research had been confirmed, he found that he was not impatient. After all, it was not as if they were likely to be interrupted by other divers in the course of their salvage work during the next couple of weeks.

They would remove the most valuable items first, hide them in the *Repera*'s ballast lockers and elsewhere on the ketch, unload the prizes at night onto the private plane he would charter at Mangareva, and then return here for more. He was not worried about parceling out shares. There should be sufficient booty for all, and he would see to it that enough went to the crew of the ketch so that any notion of, say, tossing him overboard and keeping it all for themselves did not have any reason to get a grip on their thoughts. Besides, he knew more about this place than did any of them. He might know more than they could see. Unless they were utterly stupid, they would want to keep him alive in order to make use of that knowledge.

He was elated to see that there were not two but three galleons—and one ship that despite its state of advanced decrepitude looked decidedly Chinese. A load of Ming porcelain—now that would be a treasure indeed! As for the other, more recent shipwrecks, they could hold all manner of lucrative cargo. But it was the prospect of finding older vessels that had drawn him here, and it was those antique craft that understandably now captured the greater part of his interest.

One galleon in particular seemed to be in much better shape than the others. Unfortunately, it teetered on the steep-sided edge of the seamount. Even at this depth there was the danger that a particularly strong storm surge might send it toppling over into unreachable depths.

He reassured himself that since it had laid thus for hundreds of years he was probably worrying unnecessarily. Signaling to Santos and to the other diver who was accompanying them, he finned off in the direction of the precariously balanced vessel.

It would be all right, he saw as he began to circle it. Its position was more stable than he had first surmised. Though lying at a sharp angle on its port side, the keel was jammed firmly against a long, narrow ridge of rock that protruded from the top of the seamount. Swimming parallel to the bottom, he swam from the bow toward the stern. Off to his right the ocean dropped away to cold, dark depths unknown.

Strange rock formation, he decided. It almost looked as if it could have been carved. That was impossible, of course. It was simply a natural limestone or lava ridge that had eroded away to form an unusually straight bulwark atop the rest of the underlying rock. He remained convinced of that until he reached the stern of the galleon. Hovering there, he was able to read the name below the great cabin: *Santa Isabella de Castillo*. Researching that name once he was back on dry land would likely tell him the ship's history and the cargo she had been carrying on her last, ill-fated voyage.

Something else at the stern caught his eye. More rock, mounded up to form a V-shaped fissure. The stern of the galleon had been wedged directly into this crevice.

How could that have happened, he wondered? It seemed too perfect, too unnaturally precise a fit to be a consequence of the unruly action of wind and wave and current. Still, it was not an impossible coincidence. Storm-driven sub-surface currents could certainly have slammed the ship hard into such a pocket of waiting rock.

It was when he saw the second galleon, and soon afterward the first steamship, jammed stern-first into exactly identical crevices that his thoughts began wandering to places that had nothing to do with treasure salvage, archeology, or the conventional history of South Pacific exploration.

Spinning around in the water, he saw that Santos had come up very close behind him. Gesturing at the third wedged ship, Roentgern formed a vee-shape with his hands, gestured at the vessel, and pushed his chin toward the vee. Santos nodded to show that he immediately grasped what the other man was striving to convey. By way of further response he gestured downward, over the side of the seamount, and indicated that Roentgern should follow. Thoughts churning, the bemused entrepreneur started to comply, but a check of his air dissuaded him. They had been exploring at depth for a substantial period of time. He had just enough air left in his tank to manage a proper slow, safe ascent coupled with a conservative safety stop at five meters.

Hovering over the side of the seamount, however, Santos kept gesturing for Roentgern to follow him downward. Roentgern shook his head. No doubt a better, more experienced diver than the Manhattan-bound entrepreneur, the captain would naturally have used less air and would have more remaining, as would the deckhand who accompanied them. A cautious Roentgern saw that the other man was excited. Reluctantly, he kicked away from the stern of the sunken steamship and followed the Portuguese to the edge, wondering what was so important that the captain felt the need to emphasize it so close to the end of the first of what would be many dives.

Instead of pausing to wait for him, captain and crewman promptly lowered their heads—and started to swim straight down.

Roentgern immediately held back. What was wrong with them? Were they suffering from a combination of exhilaration and nitrogen narcosis? Had they lost their bearings, control of their senses? He hovered in open water at the edge of the seamount as the two divers continued their rapid and inexplicable descent. If they went much deeper they would find themselves in real danger no matter how much air they had left.

That was when Roentgern saw that something was coming *up* out of the abyss.

At first he thought his eyes were playing tricks on him. It was no stretch of the imagination to envision something like that occurring at this depth, even in absolutely clear water. Weaving and working its way downward, unobstructed sunlight wove lazily intertwining patterns in the open water column. As Roentgern stared, wide-eyed, some of the patterns began to darken. Each rising shape slowly became something solid. Each was individually as big as the sunken steamship. Independent of the light that illuminated them, they writhed and twisted and coiled expectantly in the transparent, pellucid liquid. Splotches and dark streaks grew visible on the side of each ...

Tentacle.

Expelling bubbles in a violent, explosive stream, Roentgern started kicking for the surface. Santos and his companion were forgotten. If luck held, their presence might be enough to divert the ascending monster away from Roentgern. *Architeuthis,* he thought wildly as he swam for the surface. Giant squid. Or perhaps the fabled Colossal squid, slithered up from the Antarctic to graze on passing whales. Roentgern kicked as he had never kicked in his life.

He had no choice but to pause at five meters and decompress. If he did not outgas the nitrogen bubbles that had accumulated in his blood-stream, the bends would kill him as surely and as painfully as any sea monster. He forced himself not to look down, not to seek for what even now might be reaching up for him. If it came for him, better that his last conscious view was not one of hooked, flesh-ripping suckers and sharp slicing beak. Taken by the kraken, he thought wildly. What an end for a wily double-dealer from New York.

He did, however, have to periodically check his dive computer. Three minutes left on the safety stop—then two. Was it possible for a man to sweat underwater? He fought back the urge to cut short the decompress time and shoot for the surface early.

Only seconds left to go now....

He did not so much pop out of the water as breach. Flailing and kick-ing, he made it to the side of the ketch in minutes. Hands were waiting to take his weighted buoyancy compensator and tank and haul him out after them. Gasping for air, he collapsed on the warm, worn teak deck. Then it occurred to him: what if the monster came up after the boat itself? Though he had not seen its body, judging from the length of those monstrous tentacles alone it was more than big enough to drag the ketch down to its doom, like some lost, forlorn vessel in an ancient Spanish woodcut.

Rushing to the side, he peered hesitantly over the gunwale just in time to see emerging from the water right where he had come up—the captain, and his deckhand. Of the monster there was no sign.

He was there when the crew helped Santos onto the deck. Sucking in fresh, uncompressed air, the captain looked perfectly unfazed. A bewil-dered Roentgern found himself wondering if they really had encountered anything more substantial down there other than a trick of light and water.

"Did you see it?" he stammered. "Did either of you *see* it?"

"Of course we saw it." With the help of a crewman Santos started to peel himself out of his wetsuit. "What do you think I was pointing out to you?"

So perfunctory was this response that Roentgern found himself momentarily at a loss for words. "You mean, you saw that monster and you deliberately swam *toward* it? And beckoned for me to join you?"

Santos was stepping out of the suit now and left standing in his speedo. When a crewmember offered a towel, the captain waved it off. The sun would dry him.

"Beautiful, wasn't He?"

"*Beautiful?*" A stunned Roentgern could only gape. "I don't know, I didn't see more than the arms, and I didn't hang around long enough to ..." He paused in mid-sentence. His brow creased. "What do you mean, 'he'?"

"The Great Old One. He who waits dreaming. Only when rarely disturbed does He rise, and then usually only for a few precious moments." The captain's eyes glittered. "You should have followed. You would have been privy to a sight accorded so very few. I have to thank you, Mr. Roentgern. It is expensive to bring my people here to pay homage. We would have come another time anyway, but you have paid for that and more, and for that I thank you."

"Visit? Your 'people'? What the hell are you blithering on about?"

"We come here sometimes," Santos told him. "To pray. Others have come before us, and others will come after us." He gestured over the side. "They are down there, believers and unbelievers together. Sacrifices to Him who is Lord of the sunken city. No one else comes here. Few ships pass over this part of the Southern Ocean. There is no oil. There is no tuna. He is safe there in His House, dreaming the dead, until the time comes when He shall rise again."

The captain ceased the drivel. But though no more words emerged from his mouth, his lips continued to move in and out, in and out, as they had on one or two previous occasions. The curious habit reminded a suddenly startled Roentgern of a breathing fish. He started to back away. But there was nowhere to back away to, there on the deck of the sunstruck ketch in the middle of the great empty Southern Ocean.

"If you were coming anyway," he stammered, "then why did you want to risk bringing me along? I'm not part of your stupid cult, whatever it is. Not that I care. I'm only interested in the ships that are down there and their contents. You can worship your big squid god or whatever it is all you want. I'll even contribute an appropriate offering, if that will make you feel better about working on this site."

"A further offering on your part is not necessary," Santos burbled softly. "That is for His disciples to provide, at a later and appropriate time. But we are glad you are with us nonetheless."

The rest of the crew was closing in now, Roentgern saw. So quietly that he hadn't noticed. Like a shoal of sharks. Their lips began to pulse in and out, in and out, in a whispered, concerted, croaking chant, forming words in a language he did not recognize. For the first time in his adult life he was suddenly very, very scared. If only he had not been so confident in his own abilities to dominate others, if only he had taken more time to check out the credentials of the ship and its crew.

If only someone had bothered to tell him that *repera* means "leper" in the Tahitian language.

"If you don't want me to make an offering and you're not going to make one yourselves, then why do you care that I'm here with you?" he mumbled.

One of the crew, streaked and sweaty, was very close to him now. It struck Roentgern forcefully that the man smelled strongly of fish. No, that wasn't quite right. He corrected himself. The man smelled fishy.

Santos was smiling at him again. A wide smile. Too wide, in fact, for a face that Roentgern could now see was not entirely human.

"As you know, it a long way here from Mangareva, and a long way back, and we all of us get so very, very tired of whole trip eat nothing but seafood."

11 AH, YEHZ

W illiam Claude Dukenfield, 29 January 1880. The name sounds like one of his own jokes. Vaudeville performer, juggler, comedian, actor. Noted imbiber of alcoholic spirits. Verbal antagonist of Mae West in the film My Little Chickadee. Famous disparager of infants and suckers. Lover of his home town of Philadelphia. In proof of which, in the course of an interview given to the magazine Vanity Fair in 1925, when asked how he felt about the prospect of dying, or alternatively, what he wanted inscribed on his gravestone, he replied (the exact wording is the subject of some dispute), "On the whole, I'd rather be in Philadelphia."

Okay....

Archie had not known that some of the money was spoken for. Even if he had, he still might have been tempted to take it. A starving man will hesitate before stealing to eat, but an alcoholic in desperate need of a drink will swipe anything unguarded that is left for the taking.

So it was with Archie. He had paused only briefly before scaling the fence that walled off the cemetery from the street. It was two in the morning, a time that downtown was devoid of tourists and safe enough to attempt a quick snatch and grab. Having successfully worked the same location on several previous occasions, there was no reason to suppose anything would go wrong. This time something had. A concerned citizen objected to him absconding with the loose change. A citizen who happened to be very dead.

There was nothing dormant about the deceased's outrage, however. As a frantic Archie scooped up the last of the scattered coins, sending pennies and nickels bouncing and rolling across surrounding gravestones, a rapidly swelling humanoid shape writhed and coiled itself right up out of the grave that lay beneath the last forlorn dime. Ashen and angry, heavily bearded and clad in the tattered clothes of a bygone age, it howled curses in English and screams in banshee as it chased a terrified Archie back over the fence. Which is to say that Archie went over the fence. His pallid pursuer went right through it, shades of the dead being able to pass through solid objects with little difficulty.

In contrast to its ghostly owner, the heavy cane the angry specter swung at Archie possessed a disconcerting solidity. Descending in a potentially lethal arc, it connected painfully with his right shoulder and nearly brought him to the ground as he frantically shoved the purloined coins deeper into his pockets. For the life of him Archie could not imagine what he had done to provoke the horrific response from the usually indifferent earth. Why now, why on this night, had one of the long interred chosen to rise up and come after him? What aspect of his early morning theft had transpired differently?

None of that would matter if the phantasm, or boogeyman, or ghost, or whatever kind of horror it was that was hot on his heels actually caught up with him. His throbbing shoulder was testament to that. If that flailing spectral club came down on his head....

A sensible person might have considered giving back the money. But a sensible person did not filch coins from national monuments in the middle of a chill November night. Archie needed to live, yes, but in order to live he needed to drink. He needed to drink more than he needed to eat. He hung onto the pocketfuls of coins and kept running.

Not many people chose to stroll the streets of downtown Philadelphia at two in the morning. Those who did and happened to encounter the hysterical Archie saw a young man older than his years, unkempt and cheaply clad, running pell-mell down Church Street toward the river while looking constantly back over his shoulders. Presuming him to be afflicted by some possibly dangerous variant of the DT's, the other nocturnal walkers understandably gave him a wide berth.

"Give me back me money, y'no good thief! I'll break yer bones, I swan

I will!" Cane held high, the outline of the ethereal specter feathered slightly as it rounded a corner before condensing itself once more.

Not in the best of health to begin with, Archie raced on. In the absence of wind, muscle tone, or conditioning, he could only rely on fear to give strength to his pounding legs. Now his limited reserves were beginning to dissipate.

A light gleamed just ahead, the warm inviting glow of a bar open even at this hour. Another time Archie might have wondered at its staying open so late. Now he saw only a potential refuge from the cold, forbidding streets and the inexorable wraith that continued to close the distance between them. But even if he ducked inside, what was there to prevent his pursuer from following? He would find himself cornered. Worse, any barkeep working at this inhospitable hour would be in no mood to give shelter to an obvious drunk. He had to make a decision fast: run on past or go inside?

The figure standing just outside the doorway settled the matter for him. Puffing away on a fat cigar, the smoker's attention was understandably drawn to the oncoming Archie. Sizing up the situation, the portly figure straightened. His voice was somewhat grating, and his words oddly drawn out, but it was their content rather than their context that persuaded Archie.

"Over here, boy! Get in behind me!"

Archie did not have to be told twice. Completely out of breath as well as options, he stumbled to a halt behind the hefty figure and tried to shrink himself into invisibility. In the event of catastrophic confrontation he could still try hiding inside the open bar.

Confronted by this unanticipated interposition, the ghostly figure of Archie's pursuer slowed to a halt, his cane still held threateningly high in one half-skeletal fist.

"What manner of interference is this?" it hissed. "This be no business of yours, sor, and I'll thank ye t'mind yer own business and stand aside so that justice may be done in this matter!"

"All in good time, my good man, all in good time." The cigar migrated from one corner of the smoker's mouth to the other. He glanced briefly back down at the malnourished youth cowering behind him. "Now then, what's this pitiful young man done to merit such blatant hostility? Not that I've any inherent objection to the deliverance of a good beating, but there ought to be cause."

"Cause?" Grimacing, the hovering shade revealed ragged, broken teeth, the consequence of primitive early dental hygiene combined with some two hundred plus years of slow disintegration. "'Tis cause ye want, is it?" Lowering the cane, he angrily shook the tip in the direction of the cowering Archie. "Stole money that were given t'me by the good people of this city, he did! Helped himself to it without so much as a by-your-leave!"

Again, the stout smoker looked back at the younger man trembling behind him. "Is what this memory of a man says true, m'boy?"

Archie hesitated, then found himself nodding miserably. "Yes—yes, I took some coins. I've been doing it for a long time and nothing ever happened, ever!" He peered out from behind his protector. "I don't know what I did different tonight."

Adjusting the high hat he wore, his sapient shielder nodded sagely. "Well then, m'boy, just give this decrepit dozer his money back and be done with it, yehz? If it's just food that you need, or a temporary roof over your head ..."

Abandoning himself to confession, Archie did something remarkable. He told the truth. "I can't—I can't do that, sir. I—you see, I haven't had a drink in *days*." He licked his lips to emphasize his discomfort. "I've got the shakes real bad, and I just—I can't."

His protector's eyes widened slightly. "A drink is what you need, is it? Ah, yehz. Why, that changes everything." He turned back to the floating, and increasingly impatient, eidolon. "Have you no sympathy for the lad, then, my good man? Have you no understanding, no compassion? Why, what we are confronted with here is nothing less than a crisis of the human spirit! Why, not to assist the lad would be to deny the very essence of his humanity, yehz!"

The cane threatened. "I want the money he took off me grave!"

"Is it not better to ..." The smoker paused. "Wait just a moment now. Off your grave, you say?" He looked back at the wretched figure crouched down behind him. "M'boy, did you plot to steal coins off this man's plot?"

"I always take money off Franklin's grave," a reluctant Archie confessed. "It's mostly pennies, which are supposed to bring the thrower luck, but not everybody knows that. Lots of times they throw dimes and nickels, and sometimes quarters." His expression brightened ever so slightly. "Sometimes you can scrape together enough for a bottle!"

His interlocutor nodded understandingly, then raised a hand and pointed at the waiting wraith. "I ask you now, m'boy: does this desiccated rag of suppurating degraded flesh in any way resemble the noble Franklin?"

"Hey, just a minute now ..." the apparition began angrily.

Peering out from behind one of the older man's legs, Archie regarded his pursuer hesitantly. "Uh, no. No, he doesn't."

The cane shook violently in their direction. "My name is Thaddeus James Walker, you young fool! Mayhap old Franklin doesn't care about the coins that the credulous fling onto his gravestone, but I care about the ones that come my way. You've no right to take them!"

"Ah yehz," Archie's savior muttered under his breath. "Saving up for a glorious spending spree in the hereafter, are we? Planning to open an account at the Philadelphia Savings and Loan for the Long Demised?"

"Well ..." The drifting phantom looked suddenly confused. "That be beside the point. Theft is theft!"

"Yehz, yehz, I do not question your overall analysis of the situation, my friend. But can you not make an exception for this poor lad you see shivering behind me, of whom I suspect is about to pee in his pants? Take it from one who knows, sir, his need is dire as it is true. Can you not leave him free to indulge himself this one night? You have my personal assurance the offense shall not be repeated."

The flickering, cane-wielding shadow hesitated. Then he lowered his weapon. "Well—all right. But just this one time." He shook the heavy stick in Archie's direction and Archie flinched, drawing back behind his protector. "I'll do it on your word, William. But only this one time. If I ever see him stealing from me again I'll cave his skull in. You can be assured of that!"

Having delivered those final words of warning, the shade of the long-dead and much desiccated Thaddeus James Walker whirled about and did not so much stride off into the darkness as evaporate into the chill air of night.

Shaking as much from need as fear, Archie slowly straightened. "I—I don't know how to thank you, sir! I—was that a real ghost?"

An arm swung around Archie's shoulder as his new friend guided him toward the beckoning doorway.

"What's real and what's imaginary, m'boy, often stumble across one another in a burg as old as this. As for thanking me, why, you can buy me a drink. Have your illegitimate nocturnal perambulations garnered you enough lucre for that?"

Archie licked his lips. All he had were the coins he had managed to scrabble together. But—he owed this man his life. "I'll make sure there's enough."

"Excellent—yehz!" They entered the bar. Though well-lit, it was deserted and silent save for the clink of glasses as the bartender cleaned and stacked. He eyed Archie briefly, then smiled at the older man, who was obviously a regular.

"What'll it be tonight, Bill?"

"Something celebratory, yehz, to wish this young man well. Whiskey, as good as you can muster. In other words, something dispensed from a bottle with a label." Beaming behind a bulbous nose that Archie could now see was rosy as the blush on a Catholic high school girl's cheeks, the man set his cigar aside. "And you, m'boy—what'll you have to celebrate your survival to drink another day?"

"Whiskey also. Straight up." Digging into a pocket of his worn jeans, Archie pulled out a handful of coins and dumped them on the counter. The alert bartender kept any from fleeing. There were a lot of quarters this time, and by the tail end of the third shot Archie felt comfortable enough with his savior to put an arm around him. Luckily he was by now too tired and too drunk to freak when instead of being halted by the expected bone and muscle his lowering arm passed completely through his new friend to emerge in the vicinity of his portly but decidedly insubstantial waist.

Archie was not so inebriated that his eyes failed to widen slightly.

"Ah, c'mon—c'mon now! Don't go telling me you're a gheest—a ghost, too?"

Raising his half-full shot glass high, his savior offered a salute. "William Dukenfield's the name, m'boy, and I can't deny that I'm little more than a shade of my true self. How else d'you think I succeeded in deterring the homicidal wraith that pursed you? Takes one to persuade one, yehz." He gestured at their surroundings. "This present existence is my blessing and my curse, you see, because it's nothing less than the very one I repeatedly asked for when I dwelt among the living. It was just a recurrent joke then. Well, the joke's been on me ever since, yehz, but to its credit I have to confess it's not been a bad one." He downed the remaining contents of the glass in a single swig.

"Another one, Bill?" the bartender asked quietly.

W.C. Dukenfield studied the counter. "Alas, my noble dispenser of aged and purified grains, I fear that our young visitor here has at last exhausted his night's takings."

"This one's on the house," the bartender responded, smiling. He eyed Archie. "You too, son."

Wavering slightly, Archie started to respond instinctively—and hesitated. "Two ghosts in one neat—in one night. Thas two too many. Maybe —maybe I ought to cut back a little, y'know? I mean, the next time it might not turn out so well for me, y'know?"

"Ah, my boy," Dukenfield declared brassly, "it would be a shame to lose you to the clutches of that stolid whore sobriety. Conversely, you're a bit too young to be following in such footsteps as mine. Take it from one who knows, you really might consider drying out for a bit. Get a life first, so to speak, and then decide at your leisure how much cleansing lubrication it really requires."

Archie took a step back from the bar. "I—I'll do it! I'll go to the Shelter tomorrow and sign up for counseling. I've been meaning to, for months. All I needed was a reason. Something to push me." He shook his head, as if trying to return it to reality. "Ghosts—two ghosts. No more for me. No more. I need to"—his eyes came up to meet those of his savior —"I need to get a life, yes."

"An occupation much overrated, in my opinion," his spectral and slightly sloshed friend declared with conviction, "but then no one ever paid much attention to my opinion. Only to my jokes, yehz. Good luck to you then, m'boy, and if you should ever find yourself in the neighborhood again, be sure to drop by to share a tipple. You're buying." He turned away as the barkeep set a freshly filled shot glass down in front of him.

Suffused with unexpected resolve, Archie turned away. He needed no stiff-necked counselor to tell him that if he found himself being pursued by a ghost, much less spending a convivial evening with one, it was time to get off the bottle. His life hadn't always been like this. He just needed something to kick-start conviction again. Something as elemental and convincing as being chased down dark streets by an angry ghost, and then finding himself sharing drinks with a more amiable one.

At the door he paused to look back.

"You said—you said that this existence was one that you asked for." Raising a wavering but slowly steadying hand, he gestured at the interior of the establishment. It struck him then that the décor was—period. '30s or maybe '40s, he decided. "How does—how does one die and end up in a place like this? In a bar."

"A bar?" Taking a short slug from his freshly filled glass, Archie's rescuer focused beady but intense eyes on the younger man standing in the doorway. "Why, it's not just the bar, m'boy! I roam where and when I please. Otherwise I'd not have known your intemperate pursuer. There are quite a lot of us in this town, you know. After awhile one gets to make the acquaintance of many of one's own kind. Franklin now, he tends to keep to himself. Taking apart a computer these days, I believe. But on the right nights some of the rest of us often get together and have a little party, yehz. When he's not engaged in his profession of being a genius, old Ben likes his beer.

"What happened to me, not that you need or deserve to know, was that for years people kept asking how I felt about death and dying, so in a little piece I yammered for *Vanity Fair* back in '25 I declared, more or less, that on the whole, I'd rather be in Philadelphia. Yehz." For a second time he raised his glass in salute. "And do you know what? When I shuffled off this immoral mortal coil on Christmas Day back in '46, I found myself not in Heaven, not in Hell, not even in Los Angeles, where they finally did inter the sodden remains of yours truly. And it's here I've been ever since. Good luck to you now, m'boy, and remember one thing always: keep well clear of children and dogs."

"I'll do that, sir, and—thanks." With that, Archie went out of the bar. But not into the Wilderness. And he was forever thereafter a happy man for never forgetting that singular night's advice.

12 GREEN THEY WERE, AND GOLDEN-EYED

I've *already mentioned that my wife collects frogs. Not live frogs, but simulacra. Stone frogs, wooden frogs, painted frogs, musical frogs, gemstone frogs. For our twenty-fifth wedding anniversary, I had, via the auspices of the German scientific organization* Biopatenshaften, *a newly discovered species of Bolivian rainforest frog named after her (look up* Hyla Joanna, *if you're curious).*

But after decades of marriage and acquiring souvenir frogs for her from visits to dozens of countries, one starts to run out of options. Anyway, I can never top that twenty-fifth anniversary gift.

What I can do, occasionally and if the situation combines with the necessary inspiration, is rivet (or ribbet*) a suitable batrachian into a story. For a Christmas present, for example. Particularly fitting in this instance as we once spent a Christmas Eve day at a restaurant called FROGS, in the town of Kuranda, Queensland, Australia. The turkey wasn't great, but the unpublicized twilight flight of thousands of flying foxes more than made up for that. The restaurant is still there, I believe.*

The moon was near to full, the rain was falling unheavy and warm, and Weipo thought it an altogether fine night when he heard the crash.

At first he thought it was a tree falling, because falling trees were generally what made crashing noises in the forest. But the more he considered it, the less it reminded him of a tree falling and the more it suggested something else. Since he could not think of anything else that could cause such a loud crashing noise, he decided to set off and see for himself. This he did by vacating with a most prodigious leap the branch he had chosen for his evening perch.

As he neared the origin of the sound he began to advance more cautiously, every sense alert to the natural sounds of the forest around him and the possible presence of food. Once, he struck at a dragonfly, but missed. Disappointed, he continued on, until he came to a place where there was a hole in the canopy. Palm fronds and vines were strewn about the ground, forming a damp green halo in the moonlight around the thing which had brought them crashing down from the heights.

It was a twice-peculiar sight. Attached to a large boxy object, obviously man-made, were eight—no, nine—of the strangest creatures Weipo had ever seen. They resembled nothing so much as skinny-legged wallabies with horns. Each was fastened in harness to the boxy affair.

A very large, very rotund human was going from one creature to the next and releasing each in turn from its harness. As he did so, the animal would stagger and stumble a little ways into the forest. There it would pause, collapse, and be violently ill. Being a naturally sympathetic sort of fellow, Weipo felt sorry for them. He also felt sorry for the man, who clearly was more than a little tired and frustrated. Something told him that it would be safe to approach. If he was wrong, he was confident he could dodge any human so large.

The man was seriously overdressed in a heavy red suit with black belt and white trim. As Weipo drew near, the tall figure was exchanging a white-trimmed red cap for a rich red, wide-brimmed rain hat. He observed silently as the human drew a matching red slicker over his plush red suit. At about that time the man noticed him.

"Well, hello there. What are you grinning at?"

"I am a golden-eyed green tree frog," Weipo replied evenly, more than a little surprised at the man's ability to converse. "We're always smiling."

"I see." The large human pursed his lips, which were nearly hidden by a vast white beard that cascaded down his chest. "And I suppose it's always raining here?"

Weipo blinked. "That's why they call it a rain forest."

"I know, I know." The man sighed. "I was being facetious. You don't have to state the obvious."

Weipo nodded in the direction of the nine horned wallabies who were busy being sick all over the place. "You seem to have a problem with your animals."

"You don't know the half of it." The man consulted his wristwatch. It was a very unusual watch. Most watches are based on Greenwich Mean Time. This one was calibrated according to Christmas Mean Time. It ran slow, oh so very slow. So slow that to anyone but its owner it would have appeared dead. But it was running.

"My busiest night of the year," he said, "and look at this mess." He indicated the horned wallabies, who if anything were certainly more unhappy than their driver.

"What happened?" Weipo inquired solicitously.

"Some kind of food poisoning, I think." The man flicked a raindrop from his bulbous nose. "They have a very special diet, but no matter how careful you are this sort of thing is going to happen from time to time. It's just that it's never before happened on this particular day." He glanced down at Weipo. "I am badly in need of some provisional assistance." He hastened to explain.

So warm and needful was his expression that Weipo felt compelled to do what he could to help. As he confessed, that wasn't likely to be much.

"I'm sorry. I'd like to be of assistance, but as you can see, I'm small enough to fit in the palm of your hand."

The man nodded resignedly. He was sitting on the lower part of the boxy vehicle, his hands on his knees. "No harm in asking. There aren't likely to be any reindeer within several thousand miles of here, either."

"Is that what those things are?" Weipo regarded the unhappy horned creatures with interest. "I'm afraid not. I have, however, been giving the matter some thought, and there is one who might be able to help."

The man raised his head, a hopeful look on his face. "If you can do anything, anything at all, I promise you all the flies you can eat for life."

"That's all right." Weipo's smile grew even wider than usual. "I can manage. I'd just like to help someone who's in trouble. You stay here and I'll be back as quick as I can."

The man sighed and gestured toward the dripping Alexandra palms, from which rangiferian retching noises continued to come. "As you can see, I'm not going anywhere soon."

Weipo took off back through the forest, trying to remember where he'd last seen Mullgarra. The king of the tree frogs moved around a lot, checking on his kingdom, but Weipo had encountered him not two days earlier, exploring the billabong which had formed from a branch of the big creek.

Conscious of the sense of urgency inherent in the human's plight, he traveled as fast as he dared. Once, an amethystine python nearly got him, its sharp teeth nicking the webbing of his right foot. Another time an insomniacal emu tried to catch him by the head, but he darted left just in time and left the huge flightless bird spitting out a beakful of moist dirt.

The billabong was beautiful in the moonlight. Above the soft patter of the rain striking the glassy water the sounds of night-birds and insects could be heard, as well as the deeper-throated calls of his relations.

He found Mullgarra sitting on a flat brown rock that protruded only an inch or so above the surface. There was nothing about him to indicate that he was the king of the tree frogs, provided one discounted his slightly larger size and the small jeweled gold crown that occasionally winked into existence out of the Dreamtime and onto his head.

"Bother this thing," Mullgarra groused as he reached up to straighten the crown. "I wish it would stay or go as destiny sees fit. This coming and going of an object atop one's head is interminably frustrating." Gold eyes regarded Weipo, who floated patiently in the water nearby. "Well don't just lie there; get up here on this rock and state your business."

"Yes, your Greenness." Weipo crawled out onto the cool wet stone and settled his legs beneath him. "It's about ..."

"Excuse me." Mullgarra had spotted a juvenile salt water crocodile approaching. It was about three feet long and at the anxious frog-hunting stage. The king performed some quick calculations and parted his mouth. His tongue struck the startled croc square in its left eye, a not unimpressive feat considering that they were still some twenty-six feet apart. The croc paused, its dim reptilian mind attempting to make some sense of this impossibility, and then turned and with steady sweeps of its muscular, armored tail, swam away, blinking repeatedly.

"Sorry about that." Mullgarra returned his attention to the supplicant. "What can I do for you?"

"Not for me, your Omnipotent Olivineness. It's a human who needs your help."

Mullgarra blinked. "A human? Why should I do anything to help a human? Their children catch us and put us in jars and sometimes they dissect us. As if their own insides weren't sufficiently interesting."

"I don't think he's an ordinary human. He came crashing down into the forest in a big red box pulled by nine flying horned wallabies, only they're not wallabies, and they're not in any kind of shape to pull their own tails right now. That's his problem. He promised that if I helped him I'd have all the flies I could eat." Weipo paused, thinking if there was anything else he could add. "I know a little about humans, and I don't think this one would ever put one of us in a jar."

The king mulled this over. "First time I ever heard of a human showing a gourmet interest in flies. He sounds interesting, your plummeting acquaintance." Mullgarra glanced skyward, rain running down his bulging golden eyes and green back. "Too nice a night to sit here and do nothing except bedevil crocs. This sounds like it might be noteworthy. Where is he to be found, your human?"

Weipo turned and gestured with his tongue. Mullgarra nodded. "You say there were nine of these pulling wallaby-be-likes?" It was Weipo's turn to nod. "Very well. There's me and thee already. Go and round up seven of the guys and meet me at the place." Before Weipo could say anything more Mullgarra was on his way with a leap that carried him clear across the billabong and well into the trees beyond, the moonlight sending a pellucid shaft of light glinting off his crown.

He found Boomooloo, Nirra, and Tug in the next billabong, and Girrarree in the little stream that fed it. Ngamalgeah and Widbagar were sharing a fat grasshopper beneath a fallen fern tree, and they picked up sleepy Mauk on the way back.

They found King Mullgarra and the big round human engaged in earnest conversation by the side of the man's open-topped conveyance. Mauk was reluctant to participate, having once had an uncle smushed by an errant four-wheel drive, but Weipo convinced him it was safe by pointing out that the boxy vehicle had no wheels.

"Greetings," said Weipo cheerfully as he hopped forward. "These are me mates." The six behind him ribbetted in chorus. "I see that your situation isn't much improved."

"I'm afraid it isn't," the man admitted. "Donner is flat on his flank, Cupid is downright hoarse, Prancer is nearly as green as you are, and Blitzen is, well, blitzed. The rest aren't much better." He glanced down at Mullgarra, who was sitting on his knee. "You really think you can help?"

"Well now, as I see it, and I see quite well out of these eyes, what we have here is a little problem of spacetime. If you are telling me true that you can handle the time, I believe we can assist you in doing something about the space."

The man's lips tightened. "Believe me, I would be grateful, as would a great many children. But I don't see how you can do much."

"There are nine of your horned pullers. There are nine of us."

"There is some difference in size," the man said politely. "Also in perceived aeronautical aptitude."

"You underestimate us. People are always underestimating frogs." Mullgarra turned to his subjects. "I am going to teach you the puffing trick. It's a very old trick, a Dreamtime trick, and it hasn't been used in quite a while. Now's as good a time as any.

"What you must do is inhale and puff yourselves up, only instead of chirruping as you normally do, just keep holding and puffing, puffing and holding."

"'Scuse me," said Boomooloo, "but there's the little matter of breathing while we do this."

"Vastly overrated," sniffed Mullgarra. "Don't worry about it and it won't bother you. I'll make certain of that." He hopped off the man's knee to face the green semicircle of others. "Just watch me and do as I do. And don't breathe until I tell you to or all will be for naught. Now then —inhale!"

The heavyset man had seen many impressive sights in his time and his travels, but he had to confess that what he witnessed that night there in the rain forest ranked right up near the top.

"Bless my jolly old soul," he murmured in astonishment when Mullgarra and the rest turned to face him. Then he moved to set them in harness, placing Weipo in front in the position of honor.

When all was in readiness he climbed back into his vehicle and surveyed his extraordinary new team. There was no need presently for a lambent red nose at the front because those great golden eyes shone like searchlights in the glow of the full moon. He sat down heavily and chucked the reins. "Ready whenever you are. We've a lot of stops to make." He spared a glance for the sickly quadrupeds off to his left. "And while we're gone, the lot of you might try eating some grass."

Mullgarra glanced around and because he was king, managed the difficult task of speaking without breathing. "She'll be right, mate. Ready then? On three, mates. One, two, three ... breathe!"

The people who lived in the rain forest were used to thunder. Besides, it was late and most of them slept through it anyway. But in Ayton and Wujal Wujal a few were still awake and they heard, and where more than one sat or lay together they discussed the noise. Very peculiar sounding thunder it was, they allowed. Not a *crrraash*, or a *brrrooommm*, or even a sharp crack. Most decidedly, yes, more like an enormous, reverberant, echoing *buuurrr-aaaarrrrppp!*

After deciding that, they went about their tasks or back to sleep and forgot all about it.

Down the coast the sleigh shot, making haste along a time line stretched out like an infinite rubber band. Over the tablelands, disturbing the flying foxes. Into the small towns of the Outback and back over the larger towns of the Inback. Criss-crossing New South Wales and the big cities, thence west to Adelaide and beyond.

Skimming low over the Spencer Gulf a patrolling Great White Shark lifted its pointy snout out of the water long enough to latch onto the sleigh's left rear runner. It hung on grimly, slowing it down, as the driver dumped whatever lay on top of his bottomless bag onto the persistent fish. Eventually it became tangled up in a knot of flashing, blinking Christmas lights and let go, allowing the sleigh to regain altitude.

Being waterproof and self-powered, the lights remained lit. Frustrated, the Great White cruised the surface, blinking and winking cheerily as it made its way across the Gulf, the laughing-stock of every Great White for two hundred miles around until the integrated batteries in the light strand finally ran down.

On up through Andamooka and Coober Pedy, swinging sharply through Alice Springs and south once more, over the Nullarbor toward Perth. Then north all the way to the Kimberlys and the Bungle Bungles, turning east through Arnhem Land, the great golden-eyed frogs pulling the sleigh and its load in leaps large and bounds bitty.

It was when the Down Under circuit was nearly complete that the sleigh's driver grew, just for an instant, the slightest bit careless. It was over Burketown, still very late indeed, when Mr. Paddy Wheaton and his friend Theos happened to look up at precisely the propitiate moment. They had been spending the night engaged in a serious debate over the merits of Foster's Lager versus Four X and while their perceptive abilities were qualitatively reducio, the absurdium manifested itself only when Paddy happened to glance skyward.

His mouth dropped and his eyes bulged, though not as much as those of the creatures he saw.

"Gawd help us! There be frogs in the moon!"

Whereupon he set to running madly, and it was two days before Theos and the rest of his friends found him cowering in a bog beneath a giant lily pad, giggling at nothing in particular and stone cold sober.

Over the Top End then, descending rapidly, even at that critical moment not forgetting the children at isolated stations like Strathgordon and Merapa and Sundgrave. Back to the rain forest with its luxurious warm drizzle and night sounds, where nine anxious and extremely embarrassed reindeer waited in the unfamiliar woods.

Touchdown was, as it had been on rooftops and in farmyards, abrupt but tolerable. At a word from Mullgarra the frogs in harness exhaled relievedly, and rapidly shrunk down to their familiar, palm-sized dimensions.

"You did well," Mullgarra assured them.

"Because of you a great many nice children will not wake up tomorrow disappointed," the man told him. "If there's anything I can do for you, anything you need ..."

"*Bwarp.* Don't need a thing. I'm a tree frog, and a tree frog's life isn't such a bad one, fair dinkum. Especially if you're the king." Whereupon Mullgarra turned and in a single bound vanished into the surrounding leaves. "I'm hungry," Murk announced, and promptly hopped off into the forest. He was followed by the rest of his mates, all bounding off in different directions. All except one.

"What can I do for you?" the man asked as he worked busily to reharness his recovered (but still slightly bilious) team. "I did promise you all the flies you could eat, didn't I?"

"And if I recall correctly, I was ambivalent," Weipo replied. "There is one thing, though."

The man paused and bent over, offering the bright green amphibian the most wonderful wide smile in the world. "Name it."

Weipo looked slightly embarrassed, a difficult thing for a tree frog to bring off. "It's just that I've watched men and some of the things they can do, and while a tree frog can't hope to match them—we have no hands, for example—I thought maybe there might be a way I could do this." He beckoned and the man bent way, way down in order to put his ear close to the frog's mouth.

The beetle was big, fat, and bright yellow with black spots. It sat on its branch and rubbed its antennae together, confident it was safe despite the presence of the frog in the bush nearby.

Weipo gauged the distance, tensed his tongue, and flicked. The thin, sticky-tipped organ shot out, bent ninety degrees around one branch, ducked beneath another, described a french curve through a hole in a palm leaf, and in defiance of every known rule of amphibian physiology, whacked the startled beetle smack on the head. It recoiled sharply, retracing the same quite impossible path, to conclude its roll-up back in the tree frog's mouth.

That was interesting, Weipo mused as he munched on his snack. Later he would have to see if he could transcribe a Mobius strip.

He turned on his branch, securing a new grip with his oversized feet as he settled down to regard the moon. Around him the creatures of the tropical night scuttled and crawled and sang. Inhaling sharply, he added his own distinctive *bwarp* to the chorus, smiling with satisfaction.

Hot and sticky and steamy the rainforest might be, but for the remainder of the night it would be alive with the sound of Christmas.

13 THE DOOR BENEATH

*T*he setting for this tale is real. I wish it wasn't. On the day I visited, it was warm, sunny, with a bright blue sky dotted with occasional white cumulus. The forest through which one passes to reach the location is thick and verdant. There is no traffic save the vehicle you are in and possibly one coming the other way. There are occasional animals to be seen and many birds, but it is very quiet.

There are a few towns in the immediate vicinity. They are also quiet. Dead quiet. At the destination you are given a talk, and advice, and told what you may do and what you may not. Wandering off is among the definite no-nos. Not that, after the talk, anyone would really want to. There used to be more people here, and laughter, and love. All gone now. All as dead and gone as that portion of the woods known as the Dead Forest. The trees there are leafless, lifeless, and burned—but not by fire. By something worse.

A perfect setting for a story such as this....

It did not matter that Arkady Koslov felt secure in his job as Director of Security and Safety for the plant. It did not matter that he had been present for its initial commissioning in 1977. It did not matter that he had friends in high places. It did not even matter that Yefrem showed up in his office unannounced.

What did matter were the two men who accompanied his nominal superior. They wore similar dark suits, tinted glasses, and even darker expressions. Had they worn little plastic nameplates over their breast pockets that read "KGB" their employer could not have been more readily identified.

It helped that Yefrem smiled. "You should see the look on your face, Arkady Vitalovich. Relax, my friend. While this is a professional visit, it is not of the kind that need worry you."

Deciding to accept on the face of it what might or might not be the truth, largely because he had no choice, Koslov remained seated at his desk while gesturing his visitor to a nearby chair.

"Tea? Biscuit?"

The colonel shook his head. A champion long-distance runner in his youth, he was still whippet-thin. The incongruous walrus mustache that dominated his face like a pair of mating African caterpillars was intended to distract the attention of the follicularly sensitive from his polished bald pate. Combined with his lean muscularity this gave him the appearance of a human arrow; one capable of piercing the unwary or the guilty at a moment's notice. In contrast, his broad smile was disarming; intentionally so.

Studying them, no one would have assumed he and Koslov worked for the same national department, taking their orders directly from Moscow. Where in appearance the colonel was as threatening as a dyspeptic Cossack, the Director was avuncular. The consumption of too many blini had ballooned his own once-athletic body. Where years ago he had played serious rugby, his gut now closely resembled a rugby ball. His own hair was thinning, undecided whether to continue the fight to cover his head or give up entirely. He was not blubbery; just soft. A secure desk job will do that to a man.

At least, he assumed it was still secure.

"If I am not to be worried, you need to explain the necessity for your garrulous escort."

Yefrem nodded toward the large man on his left. "A procedural requirement. I am going to show you something, and it is not permitted that I do so without suitable accompaniment." He leaned forward and lowered his voice slightly. "It is really not necessary, but you know how Moscow is."

Knowing too well, Koslov did not even bother to nod. "I am to come with you now, to see this 'something'?"

"Now," Yefrem told him. "So we can arrive before the test begins. It has been decided that considering your position and your unmarred record of service you deserve to know what is happening." He winked. "I pushed for it."

Koslov was finally starting to relax. It did not matter that Yefrem was not a friend: only that he was not an enemy.

"The test is routine. It has been performed before. Why the interest now?"

Yefrem shook his head. "The test to which you are referring is not the same as the one to which I am going to show you. I refer to another, involving a different portion of the facility. One with which you are unfamiliar."

The Director frowned. "I consider myself familiar with every corner of the plant."

"Then prepare to be enlightened, comrade Koslov."

The lift that was located between components three and four of the facility was well known to the Director. It was one he had ridden hundreds of times. Entering behind the colonel and flanked by the two KGB guards, he turned to watch as Yefrem removed a silvery tag and passed it over the lower, buttonless corner of the lift's gold-toned control panel. The tag, he noticed, was attached to the colonel by a metal chain.

Mentally timing the journey, he soon realized they were descending well below ground level. That in itself was interesting because the lowermost button on the elevator control panel stopped the lift at the surface. The plant had no subterranean levels to access. Or so he had believed.

No indicator lit up on the panel when the lift finally halted. There was nothing to indicate how far they had descended or if any additional unknown levels lay below this one.

Stepping out, he waited for Yefrem to take the lead once again. At once surprised and stunned, he found himself accompanying the colonel down a wide corridor filled with men and women intent on unknown tasks. Recognizing none of the faces, he commented on the fact to his guide.

"They come here directly from the river." The colonel was evidently enjoying his colleague's bewilderment. "There is a tunnel equipped with silent electric transport. The workers in the main facility above never see or interact with those who work down here."

"But why?" Koslov noted that many of the unfamiliar personnel were wearing lab coats. Others were draped in vests filled with small tools. "Why such secrecy, even from someone in my position?"

The colonel's voice tightened as they turned a corner. "It is deemed necessary to keep knowledge of the project from being passed to others. The Americans, the British, the Chinese—anyone. That is why it was constructed here, beneath the plant, where it is safely hidden from even the most sensitive espionage apparatus. It is the most closely guarded operation in the country, comrade Koslov—and you are about to, finally, be granted access."

The Director pondered a moment. "Why now? Why keep it secret from me for nearly ten years only to share it with me now?"

"I told you. There is to be a test." One leathery finger pointed upward. "It is no secret that a test of component four of the facility is to be conducted today. That will provide any cover necessary for the parallel experiment we are about to conduct down here."

"What kind of experiment?" Koslov's curiosity had long since overcome any fear he felt for his personal safety.

"You will see. All of us will see, at the same time."

They had reached a door. It should not have been there. The entire subterranean level should not have been there. Even as Yefrem showed identification to the guards flanking the doorway, who gripped modified AK-47s with a determination rarely seen outside of Lubyanka, the Director marveled at the portal. Made of alloyed steel, it looked more like the door to a vault in a major bank than anything one would expect to find beneath the plant.

Once clearance had been granted one of the guards spoke into the microphone clipped to his collar. A moment passed, the guard nodded to no one in particular, and then the barrier swung inward on hinges the size of refrigerators. The wall it penetrated was two meters thick and made of the same specially reinforced concrete as much of the regular facility above ground.

Koslov's eyes widened as he followed the colonel into the room beyond. He could not help himself. The chamber they entered was high, wide, and deep enough to hold large aircraft. Ranks of powerful ceiling lights poured illumination on the area below, penetrating every corner of the vast open space. The deep-throated background whine of concealed fans explained the slight breeze he felt on his face. The room was suffused with purpose and expectation.

To the left was a semicircle of instrument banks that reminded the Director of pictures he had seen of the operations room of the national cosmodrome in Kazakhstan. Technicians sat or stood behind dozens of flickering monitors while others moved to and fro from one station to the next. In addition to Russian he heard snatches of speech in several other languages, some of which were a distinct surprise. On the other side of the chamber opposite the rank of instruments was—well, it was difficult to tell exactly what it was.

At first glance he thought it an incomplete, unfinished black sphere some two stories high. Looking closer he saw that its apparent depth was an optical illusion, albeit an extremely effective one. What at first glance appeared to be a globe on closer inspection revealed itself to be more of a hemisphere. The outer circumference was uneven and fuzzy. He rubbed his eyes. Every time he looked at the thing it appeared to change shape ever so slightly. The more solid base it rested on, or rather disappeared into, was a twisted mass of distorted gray metal. Or maybe it was ceramic in nature, he decided, or perhaps glass. Not being a materials scientist he couldn't tell, especially from a distance. Regardless of what it was made of, the interlocking, fused shapes that comprised the base were as enigmatic as abstract art, their overall appearance oddly unsettling.

He did not dwell on the singular object because fascinating as it was, it paled in comparison to the shapeless gray-green mass that dominated the center of the room. The massive uneven lump would have filled a good-sized aircraft hangar all by itself. It was featureless save for numerous dark blotches that streaked the sides. Emerging from terminals in the floor, a feathering of wires ran into and over the quiescent mass. Additionally, the entire hill-sized mound was enclosed in what at first glance appeared to be a glistening fish net, but which on closer inspection revealed itself to be made of braided wire.

So intent was a captivated Koslov on the greenish hill and the vision-distorting construct at the far end of the huge chamber that he twice tripped over cables that snaked across the floor. When he and his escort finally halted by the nearest node of linked electronic consoles, Yefrem proceeded to introduce him to a stolid, handsome woman in her early fifties.

"Comrade Koslov, this is Dr. Marian Schumenko. Doctor, Comrade Koslov is Director of Safety and Security for the ..."

"I know who he is." A narrowing stare so intense it seemed capable of igniting newsprint swept perfunctorily over Koslov before turning back to the console behind her. Ignoring the two men, either of whom had the power to order her immediate arrest or detention, she exchanged words first with the younger man seated at the console on her right before moving on to look over the shoulder of another seated at her left.

Moments passed. As if abruptly recalling the terse introduction she spoke without looking around. Her mind, Koslov could tell, was wholly focused elsewhere.

"Tell him not to touch anything." She was plainly speaking to Yefrem. "And to stay out of the way. That includes you as well, comrade Colonel."

The expression on the KGB officer's face tensed but he said nothing. His reaction was all that was necessary to tell Koslov who was really in charge here.

He looked around as lights flashed and beeping alarms began to sound. Activity, already high, intensified throughout the chamber. Men and women who had been working in immediate proximity to the hemispherical object and the looming green-gray mass moved rapidly away from both. The scientist's slight already forgotten, Yefrem leaned close to his guest and whispered.

"While the regulation test of the above-ground facility has already commenced, I can tell you that the experiment that is about to take place here is infinitely more important."

"What are you testing for?" Workers and techs continued to clear the floor. Throughout the open chamber, yellow flashing lights fastened to floor, walls, and ceiling turned to red.

"To tell you the truth, no one is really certain. But I can say that this is not the first time the great mass you see before you has been tested. A similar assessment was attempted once before, three years ago, although on a much lesser scale."

"An assessment? Of whatthat?" Koslov indicated the greenish-gray hill. "What is it, anyway? It looks like a pile of coagulated industrial sludge."

Yefrem smiled, but this time humorlessly. "We are convinced it is organic."

Koslov gaped anew at the shapeless mass. "What, that? Even a dead blue whale is not so big."

The colonel nodded. "Hence the need for proper assessment. We still do not know exactly what it is. Every attempt at straightforward dissection has failed. The epidermis, if that's what it is, appears soft, yet it cannot be cut. Not by blade, not by saw, not even with an industrial laser. Steel and ceramic break against it while a laser simply warms the area on which it is trained."

"Then how do you know it is organic?"

"A small section was raised up and inserted in a portable MRI scanner. The resultant imaging made no sense. What was observed appeared scrambled and disorganized, with no recognizable cellular structure." He nodded at the shadowy hillock before them. "Much as it all appears to be. One theory holds that it is a mélange of many far smaller creatures forced together by heat and pressure. Another, and I know this sounds extreme, but I only pass on what I have been told, is that it is something of extraterrestrial origin that survived a fall through our atmosphere. The impenetrability of its exterior would allow for such a descent. We have recovered small bits of possible organic material from meteorites. Why not something much larger?"

Koslov tried to make sense of the whirl of new information. "And what of the peculiar construction at the far side of the chamber?"

"Ah. That is an entirely different problem. Though inorganic, it is like-wise composed of unknown materials. In addition it possesses some inter-esting optical properties that our physicists continue to study."

"Let me guess." Koslov had not risen to his present position through a paucity of imagination. "Both of these enigmas were found together, or at least in close proximity to one another."

Yefrem nodded. Somewhere a siren wailed for attention. "Not simply together, but linked. By a braided cable of unique alloy. That, at least, our people have been able to analyze. Though far from perfected, the results of that research have gone a long way toward enhancing the reliability of such things as the interior lining of our biggest rocket engines."

Gazing at the drab greenish mass, Koslov asked the obvious question. "Why would two such diverse anomalies be linked together?"

The colonel shrugged. "Until we can divine the nature and possible purpose of each, none can say."

"I take it then that the previous assessment you mentioned did nothing to resolve such questions?"

"Not only did it not resolve them," Yefrem replied, "as is the case with many experiments it only raised new questions." He nodded toward the center of the chamber. "When the first overtly invasive attempts did not succeed in providing an entry into the mass, someone thought to try a high-powered electric arc cutter. This was duly acquired from the Energi-mass people and applied to the volume's exterior. Though it remained inviolate, a tiny section was seen to jump in response to the application of localized current. Subsequent attempts at other sites around the lump's perimeter produced identical responses. More importantly, with each use of the arc cutter the edges of the hemispherical object appeared to give off a brief pulse of dark light."

"Dark light?" Koslov made a face.

"That is how it was described to me. I was not present to witness it personally. I am told that photographic images taken at the time fail to replicate the phenomenon correctly." He turned to face the Director. "Even that, however, is not the most interesting or intriguing result of the initial experiment, which took place on the twenty-first of July three years ago."

Searching his memory for some happening of significance on the referenced date, Koslov came up empty. Yefrem elaborated.

"This impenetrable mass and its attendant inscrutable object were originally discovered and subsequently extracted from where they had been found buried deep within the Antarctic ice. They were then transported here via ship and in great secrecythrough the Black Sea, then up the Dnieper and into this facility via the tunnel that was constructed between here and the river." His voice fell to a murmur.

"On the same day as that first experiment three years ago, at the same time as a glow was detected from the hemispherical object, the lowest temperature ever recorded on the surface of this planet was observed. Minus eighty-nine point two centigrade. At our Vostok Station in Antarctica, not far from where these peculiar discoveries were found."

A disbelieving Koslov drew back slightly. "You're not implying, comrade Colonel, that there might be some sort of connection between the two?"

Yefrem shrugged. "It is not my job to speculate on such things. I am merely sharing the same information that was passed to me. What happened on that day may be no more than coincidence. Make of it what you will."

Though the colonel seemed as though he might have had more to say, and Koslov certainly had additional questions, their conversation was interrupted by the sounding of a warning klaxon loud enough to drown out casual conversation. After a final check of one last connection the sole technician remaining on the chamber floor hurried to his assigned station. Koslov did his best to mimic Yefrem's intensity as the colonel stared at the somber mass whose motionless bulk all but filled the expansive chamber. Nearby, Dr. Schumenko was muttering a stream of commands to the man seated before her.

The lights in the chamber dimmed. A final verbal warning was given over loudspeakers. There was a pause, then final directives were broadcast. Switches were thrown, connections made. A loud crackling sound filled the air as a tremendous jolt of electricity was passed through the cables that ran into the central mass and simultaneously electrified the net that was draped over it. Koslov felt the remaining fine strands of hair on his head twitch and his skin tingle. For certain there would be no shortage of current to deliver to the mass of presumed organic material. Not with the plant itself directly overhead.

Additional commands were given. The power was shut down. Had the edges of the hemispherical shape brightened, as they supposedly had three years ago? From his vantage point at the opposite end of the chamber Koslov could not tell.

It was quiet in the chamber, the only noise coming from the overhead air circulation equipment. Then people began to talk, to discuss, to debate. Otherwise nothing had changed. The steely Dr. Schumenko's attitude remained resolved as she continued her terse conversation with colleagues. Unaware of how tense he had become, Koslov jumped slightly as Yefrem's hand came down his shoulder.

"Quite a show, was it not?"

"Most ... most interesting." Koslov swallowed. "What happens now?"

"Now? Now we go back to work. With the exception that you are now privy to this place and to what goes on down here. If there are any actual results, I will see that any such information is passed along to you in a suitably safe format. Come, I will accompany you back to your office." He smiled. "Now I will have that tea."

Leaving behind the consoles and their busy, attendant scientists and technicians, they started back toward the main doorway. As they did so Koslov observed that a pair of technicians had gathered around one place at the near periphery of the greenish mass. They were soon joined by a third man, and then several more. Halting, he pointed.

"What's going on over there?"

Yefrem glanced in the indicated direction and shrugged. "A burned area, perhaps. Even if penetration was accomplished it is not for us to linger and wait for the analysis. If anything of interest has been found it will be duly recorded and passed along." He resumed walking.

Koslov hesitated. There seemed to be some agitation among the cluster of technicians. A moment later he heard the scream. It was the first of several.

Audible only to those in the immediate vicinity, the yelling did not immediately alert the bulk of the scientific staff. Koslov, however, was close enough to see the curve at the base of the mass from which the half dozen technicians fled. They had not been studying a burn mark, as Yefrem had casually suggested. They had been examining one of the many dark streaks that scored the hillock's flank. As the Director's mouth opened wide he saw that it was something more than a dark mark.

It was an eyelid. The technicians were fleeing from an open eye.

The revealed iris was a fiery red-orange, the pupil comparatively small and black as ink. Frozen in place, unable to move from where he was standing, Koslov saw another similar dark space higher up twitch, flutter, and open. A second eye appeared. Then a third, then two more, until the eruption of ferociously hued oculars rose like a wave across the flanks and top of the great mass. The chamber was filled with screams now. Scientists were rising from behind their consoles to point excitedly while lesser techs were scrambling at their instrumentation.

Magnified by the enclosed space, a great groaning sound echoed throughout the chamber, a metallic creaking as of an enormous weight being shifted. As the stunned Koslov stared, the huge compendium of organic material moved slightly. No, he told himself. It was not a compendium. What he now behold was a single organism flecked with ever-increasing numbers of multiple eyes each of whose inhuman glare was intense enough to shrivel one's soul. The sight was awe-inspiring, overwhelming, humbling. Terrifying.

Then the first mouth appeared, no rhyme or reason to its location, and extended itself pseudopod-like to inhale a staring technician who was standing too close.

That should have drawn, should have held, every bit of Koslov's attention. Instead he found himself being violently shaken. With one powerful hand Yefrem was gripping the Director's left shoulder. With the other he was pointing. Not at the rippling, heaving, increasingly animated pulpish atrocity before them, but to its right. To the far end of the chamber.

The hemispherical relic was spinning so fast that the motion was barely detectable. Purple light danced from its fringes, shards of lightning spitting off in all directions. As he gawked at the geometrically obtuse base that now pulsed with an unvarying ominous glow, Koslov found that he suddenly understood the meaning of dark light.

It was neither the refulgent base nor the spinning hemisphere that had drawn the colonel's attention, however, but what was becoming visible within. It was a depth, a core, a penetration into Somewhere Else. And at the back of that unimaginable deepness something was moving. Something so vast and frightful as to make the creature that was now heaving within the frail electrical net that struggled to contain it appear as no more than an ant would to a human.

Staring at that which should not be looked upon, Koslov tried to scream and found he could not. His mouth, his vocal cords, his thoughts, were as paralyzed with fear as was the rest of his body.

Feeling himself stumbling, he turned in shock to see Yefrem peering hard at him. The colonel's expression was set, his gaze determined. In his other hand he held the pistol which Koslov knew had occupied the concealed vest holster all along. Of the two formidable escorts who had previously accompanied them there was no sign. They had fled. But not the colonel.

"Get out, Koslov! Run! Maybe you can do something!"

"Do ...?" The stunned Director fumbled for words, his attention locked on the hideously animated mass of protoplasm that shuddered in the middle of the chamber. With every moment it was growing more and more active. As he stared, additional tentacular mouths emerged from the heaving mass to snatch up another screaming technician, then another, and then Dr. Schumenko herself. She was not so proud that she failed to scream like a girl as she was sucked down and disappeared into the weaving, tooth-lined tube of flesh.

"Try!" Yefrem gestured sharply. "You see what's in there? Do you see what's lurking? That construction—it's a portal of some kind. A gate, an opening—I don't know. I'm no scientist. But I know what I see. We've opened it somehow. We've opened our world to somewhere else, somewhere horrific, and it has to be shut! Before things worse than *this* can come through!" With his free hand he shoved Koslov so hard that the Director stumbled. With his other he was already firing at the surging mass behind them.

"Do whatever you can, Koslov! Do whatever you *have* to do!"

His mind awhirl, his nerves screaming, the colonel's last words echoing in his head, Koslov fled. As he ran for the doorway he was passed by the two guards who had originally granted them entry. Courageous men, they were firing at the now moaning, gibbering mass of seemingly indestructible organism as fast as they could unload the magazines of their weapons. Their bullets, like their bravery, had no effect on it.

Then he was out in the corridor. Resolutely ignoring the cries and confusion that surged around him, he forced his way to the lift that had brought him down to what was now a warren of horror. Espying the closed door, he experienced an awful moment when he feared that the lift had been rendered inoperative. When it opened at his touch he felt a surge of relief. Only the visible buttons were necessary to activate the lift and send it rising upward. This had the added benefit of shutting out the screaming below. Wedded to their assignments, none of the bevy of confused technicians had joined him. When the full overwhelming horror of the situation below ground reached them he had no doubt there would be mass panic to reach the restricted lift, any lift, or the tunnel that led to the river, or to access any other means of transportation that might enable the staff of the secret facility to flee.

The comparative silence above ground when he emerged from the lift was shocking in its normality. Plant personnel strolled calmly about the manicured grounds. A flock of cranes from the nearby lake soared over-head. A trio of workers carrying food from the cafeteria eyed him in confusion as he ran past them, breathing hard. Ignoring calls and greet-ings he rushed to reach the site of the above ground test. A check of his watch showed that it was already well underway.

Do something, Yefrem had urged him. *Try.* But what could he do? The portal, if that's truly what it was, was open. It was linked to the immense thing that the powerful electric charge had brought back to life. Estab-lished as it was, how could he possibly close such an opening? Especially now that its guardian, or whatever, had been activated beside it?

One thing he did feel for certain. If even one of the horrors he had barely glimpsed through the open portal succeeded in squeezing its way through to this side of the opening, nothing man and all his puny devices could do would be able to force it back in again.

It was this that told him what he must do. The realization horrified him, but not as much as what he had seen below. He knew he had no choice.

His supposition was quite correct. The above-ground facility's test was in full swing when he arrived in the control room. Though startled by his somewhat wild appearance, those who knew him accepted his pres-ence without question. After all, he ranked nearly every technician present. Walking swiftly around the room, he began to issue orders. Though puzzled by some of these, the respective techs to whom he addressed instructions readily complied. In fact, they were relieved at his arrival. Properly, the test should not have been initiated without him present.

It was only when his directives began to trespass certain boundaries that this or that technician thought to take issue with them.

"Comrade Koslov," one tech muttered softly, "are you certain you wish to disable these systems?"

Koslov was more than firm in his reply. "Engineer Samsov, how can we expect to determine the ultimate safety of the system if we do not proceed to the inevitable conclusion of this test without the automatic shutdown mechanisms disabled? It is the only sure way to determine if the overall safety system in place will operate properly."

"Yes sir, I see that, but ..."

Koslov leaned close. "Don't argue with me, Samsov! Do your job. I take full responsibility."

"Yes, comrade Director." Reluctantly, the engineer moved to comply with the command.

Beneath them, the floor quivered noticeably. A number of the techs on duty exchanged uncertain glances. Someone suggested the cause might be a small earthquake. That was absurd, another objected. One reason the plant had been sited on this location was because it had been determined to be tectonically stable.

That did not prevent the floor from heaving upward again, this time at least a full centimeter. An increasingly desperate Koslov thought he could hear a distant howling, mounting in strength and intensity, though those around him thought it was only the machinery. Striving not to appear panicked, he grimly issued additional orders.

"Insert the control rods! All of them!"

A couple of the techs looked at him as if he had lost his mind. He didn't care. All that mattered was that the personnel responsible did as he commanded.

The result was as he hoped. Even as a greenish-gray pseudopod the thickness of a telephone pole thrust upward through the floor, there came a tremendous surge of power from below that had nothing to do with the awakening monstrosity from the Antarctic and everything to do with the design of the fourth component of the plant.

The interaction of superhot fuel with the overwhelmed cooling pools resulted in a shattering of the fuel itself together with an immediate increase in pressure. Striving to escape the resultant discharge of suddenly released radioactive material, the thing beneath gave a tremendous, desperate shove upward. The thousand-ton protective cover plate that shielded the upper portion of the facility strained at its foundations, was dislodged and pushed aside. Fuel channels ruptured and control rods jammed in place. As the speech of confused and now terrified technicians dissolved into an incoherent babble around him, Koslov closed his eyes. He knew what was coming.

There was an explosion of almost incalculable dimensions.

Thrown skyward, shattered fragments of shoggoth rained back down into the gaping hole, only to be utterly consumed by the towering blaze that now roared a hundred meters higher than the plant itself. As they struck the fire the organic fragments ignited, turning the flames all the colors of the rainbow. Melting downward, molten nuclear material rushed into the subterranean research facility, obliterating the portal before Something vast and evil could push its way through. That was all the obituary the dozens of scientists and technicians, the workers and guards, ever obtained. Their memories were erased as thoroughly and completely as their work.

In the depths of the Kremlin a singular secret file pays tribute to the heroes of that day. Not to the technicians who strove mightily to subdue the runaway, destroyed facility, nor the firemen who gave their lives to fight the strangely multihued blaze that erupted from its depths. Their monuments are widely known, the statues to them plainly visible to the occasional visitor to the site. Only within that sole file, hidden from the rest of the world and unknown to all save a few specially selected and carefully cleared scientists and politicians, can be found the names of such as Dr. Marian Schumenko, Director Arkady Koslov, Colonel Yefrem Andropov, and dozens of others. It is a necessary shame that their sacrifice can and will never be known to but a chosen few.

Meanwhile the greenery and wildlife has returned to Chernobyl. Limited numbers of tourists stroll its grounds, marveling at the dead town of Pripyat and gawking at the ruins of reactor #4, never knowing what once stirred beneath their fully covered feet (sandals are not allowed). Never wondering why the containment vessel is really called a sarcophagus. Though most *are* curious as to why it is in the process of being replaced by a new containment vessel of steel and polycarbonate when, despite the arguments, the old one looks perfectly capable of containing something as diffuse as mere radiation.

Unless, of course, there is something on the site other than radiation that needs to be contained.

14 CASTLEWEEP

O n the coast of Ghana there is a vast complex of cut stone called Cape
Coast Castle. Of the many such slave trading forts, or "castles," that dot
the southern coast of the bulge of West Africa, Cape Coast is perhaps
the most fully restored. Now a museum operated by the Ghanian government, one
can wander freely through the rooms, apartments, stables, storerooms, and grounds.
Lit by the equatorial sun, all is bright and light and whitewashed.

The dungeons have not been whitewashed.

There are dark paving stones on the floor, and walls scratched by the nails of
wailing human beings, and iron chains. Lots of chains. In the depths where people
stolen from their homes waited amidst filth and disease for shipment to unknown
destinations there is a grating in the ceiling through which one can see the sky. The
small circular glimpse of the world beyond is worse than the darkness.

All of Ghana is well-known and traveled. To site the worst of such horrors in
modern times requires a location less explored. The central African nation of Gabon
offers that. Slavery found its way to Gabon as well, but far less frequently than the
"Slave Coast" region farther north and west.

There was less available merchandise, but the horror was just the same.

"The walls weep, but only on nights when the moon is full."

Uh-huh, Cort mused as he cast an amused glance across the folding
camp table at Shelly. *And the gorillas dance in the clearing while the frab-
ulous chimpanzee thumps out a beat on a hollow log and the black*

colobus monkeys chorus in counterpoint from their perches high in the odum trees. Shelly's tight grin showed that she was having an equally hard time repressing a laugh. Sharing a knowing smirk with her, he decided, would have to do.

They were up in the northeastern part of the country, where Gabon fades toward the Congo and tempts the inhabitants of that unhappy country to risk an illegal dash across the border for a chance at a life in their more prosperous, less populated neighbor. Cleft by the Equator, little in the way of civilization penetrated this obscure, densely forested corner of one of the planet's least-visited countries. Baka pygmies still silently stalked downsized duiker in the depths of soundless jungle while keeping a wary eye out for dyspeptic forest elephants and the occasional fidgety lime-green mamba. If not for the unauthorized loggers and illegal bushmeat hunters probably no one would come here at all, Cort mused.

A soft rush of disturbed air as if a small plane was passing low overhead caused him to set his coffee down while casting a casual glance skyward. It was only another spectacular hornbill. He was sick of hornbills and their interminable raucous cries. It was just after noon and not much was stirring in the forest. Soon it would be too hot even for the mangabeys to move.

You knew you were in the real tropics, he reflected, when you sat perfectly still, did not move a muscle, and sweat still ran off you in rivulets. Every day, his chest became a delta.

Peering across the battered table, he found himself admiring Shelly anew. He had known many attractive women, but she was the first he had ever met who had shown a willingness to accompany him on a trip like this instead of insisting they must go somewhere like Rome or the Riviera. Her predecessors' notions of exploring the tropics rarely extended beyond attending a garden party in Miami. Limiting their horizons thusly caused them to miss out on much that was of interest.

Him, for one thing.

Where his personal appeal was concerned, Cort labored under no false illusions. The substantial trust fund he had inherited only enhanced his attraction to the opposite sex. He felt no shame at this unearned wealth. *We are none of us responsible for the conditions imposed upon us by fortuitous origins,* he had often cheerfully reminded himself. Usually while withdrawing money.

Now, as they neared the end of this particular journey, having gone about as far north in Gabon as one could go without running out of road entirely, their driver apparently felt it necessary to conclude their last day with a fairy story.

"Let me guess." Cort winked at Shelly, who had to lower her gaze to hide her smile. "You're referring to a *secret* place, and nobody knows about it but you."

Yacouba looked offended.

"Not so, Mr. Cort. Many people know about the place. They just don't go there."

Shelly could restrain herself no longer. "Oh, let me guess." She bugged her eyes and trembled her hands. "It's—*haunted*."

Their guide pursed his lips. He was a small, slightly built man from a coastal tribe, but no pygmy. In addition to being a student of local history he was also an excellent driver, a self-taught 4X4 mechanic, a decent cook, and fluent in English and French as well as an unspecified number of local languages. He was an educated man, having attended university, but family needs had prevented him graduating. He had revealed to Cort that his dream was to be a historian, but when one had an extended family to support one took what work was available.

Given the man's background, Cort would not have expected him to indulge in local superstitions.

"You joke at my expense." Yacouba was clearly hurt. "If you don't believe me, ask the Fang."

Cort started to laugh aloud, but caught himself. "The Fang? Don't you mean 'a' fang?"

The driver eyed him tolerantly. "The Fang are a large and powerful tribe in Gabon. They know the territory of which I speak better than anyone. They know full well what lies hidden among these mountains. But even they will not go to the place I tell you about now."

Cort nodded, sighed forbearingly, and took a swig from the mug sitting on the table in front of him. He'd had just about enough of camp brew and would be glad to get back to Boston and some decent coffee. Such unavoidable impositions aside, he had to admit that he had enjoyed the trip. Even if the principal motivation in embarking upon it had been to provide him with the means to yet again one-up his many sometimes insufferable globe-trotting friends. To the best of his knowledge, none of them had ever been to this part of the world. Naturally he could not resist the opportunity to beat them to it. Once home he would regale them with tales of his grand adventure while delighting in their inevitable expressions of envy.

"I suppose you're referring to some ancient, mysterious relic of a bygone race and age?" he ventured.

"No." Yacouba now spoke not as a guide but with the assurance of a scholar. "The place I speak about is only a few hundred years old. It was built by Europeans."

Cort perked up slightly. It was not the explanation he had been expecting. "Europeans? What Europeans?"

Clearly pleased to share more knowledge of his homeland, the guide continued. "No one knows for certain who came first to the place of which I speak. Given the age of the walls, most probably the Dutch. But it might have been the French, or the English, or quite possibly the Portuguese. At one time or another all of them could have had a hand in it."

Cort looked again at Shelly. While informative, their driver was still being evasive. "So at this place on the night of a full moon there are walls that weep. What kind of walls, Yacouba?"

"Stone walls. The walls of a castle."

Now that was interesting, Cort decided. Could the ruins of some forgotten British or Dutch outpost lie this far inland, beyond mountains and across forest, overgrown and concealed by centuries of festering jungle? During the great age of exploration and colonization the Europeans had built and maintained posts all along the west coast of Africa, but until the nineteenth century few of them had ventured very far into the interior. Still, big, fast-flowing local rivers like the Makokou and the Ogoou offered a route inland, just as the great Congo itself did farther to the south. What lure might have drawn early European explorers away from the coast and into the hellish, fever-infested hinterland?

There was gold in Gabon, and diamonds all over Africa. Had some undocumented explorers found and then lost a diamond mine? As for the "weeping" walls, a full moon might produce just enough of a tidal surge in a pool or river to send its water trickling over the old stone wall of a cistern or two, giving it the appearance of weeping. Or so Cort chose to surmise. He would have been the first to admit that he was no scientist. But it was the best explanation he could think of on the spur of the moment. Assuming an explanation was even called for. Yacouba might simply be yanking his chain.

He gave a mental shrug. Why not check it out? It wasn't as if he had to be back at a job or anything.

"It'll be a full moon in a few days. If you're not just spinning us a tall tale, Yacouba, I think Shelly and I would be interested in having a look at your weeping walls."

Their driver immediately looked away. "No. You are right. It is just a story, *m'sieur*. A forest fable to amuse children."

Cort grew annoyed. First, because he didn't like the guide's tone, and second, because people did not say "no" to William Edward Cort. But he did not get angry.

"Come on, Yacouba. You tell us this story, you get me to where I'm half-believing you, and then when I seek actual confirmation you decline to provide it."

As the guide turned to face him, Cort was startled to see that the man's expression was not one of defiance or uncertainty, but unmistakable fear.

"I know of this place, Mr. Cort. I mention it to you only in passing—not thinking you would ever contemplate actually going there. I know where it is supposed to lie, but I myself have never been there. I will never be there." His sudden resolve was startling.

Bored by the discussion, Shelly delicately sipped down the last of her coffee, pondered the cookies set out on a paper plate in the middle of the table, and leaned back in her folding canvas chair. "Go or don't go—I don't care, Cor. One more week of this and then we head home. That was the arrangement. I've put up with these conditions pretty well, I think." Her gaze narrowed. "You owe me a month in London. With shopping."

"I know, I know." He replied irritably and without looking at her. "Can we get to this place in three days, Yacouba?"

The driver looked away again. "One day rough driving, then two days walk. Same back out again. Not easy, but it could be done." There was no hesitation in his voice. "But it does not matter. I will not take you there. I am sorry now that I mentioned it."

Cort sighed and leaned toward the guide. He knew exactly what to do because he had done the same thing dozens of times before and it always worked. Always. "I paid you half your fee in Libreville." His smile was not unlike that flashed by the crocodiles that inhabited the nearby river. "I'd hate to have to reconsider payment of the rest following our return due to, um, unsatisfactory fulfillment of designated duties."

As expected, the threat shook Yacouba. Not only did he need the money for his family, but Cort knew how the game was played. If a Westerner filed a formal complaint with the Tourism Department in Libreville,

Yacouba could lose his official guide's license. In a country like Gabon, something like that could mark him for life.

Despite the implied threat, Yacouba still hesitated. Eventually he cursed under his breath.

"I will take you close enough to see. But I won't go to the weeping walls myself."

Cort put his hands behind his head, leaned back in his seat, and nodded complacently. "Fine. You stay with the tent and the rest of the gear. That's all we want, is to have a look." He winked at his companion. "Isn't it, Shelly?"

She did not turn back to him. A night bird was singing in the trees and she was trying to locate it. "If you say so, Cor," she said absently.

"Then it's settled." Even if they didn't find a lost diamond mine, he told himself as he pushed back from the table, there might be relics of historical value. His bank account would ensure smuggling such artifacts out of the country would pose no obstacle. It wouldn't be the first time on an overseas trip he had been compelled to hand out baksheesh. He might get his picture in the paper back home. The anticipation was delicious as he envisioned the boys at the Club pondering his triumph and fuming.

Pain made him wince suddenly. Looking down, he slapped hard at whatever had bitten his exposed calf. Something small, multi-legged, and dull blue in color scampered madly off his leg as it made for the cover of the low scrub beneath the nearby land cruiser. His momentary visitor was not close kin to what one might expect to encounter on, say, the grass of Boston Commons.

Central Africa, Cort reflected, would be a far more tolerable place without the bugs.

It was a stupid idea. The notion that it had been a stupid idea struck Cort forcefully about an hour after they had left the land cruiser parked at the terminus of a winding, bumpy, near-impassable track that could not by any stretch of the imagination truly be called a road. What kept him going now that they were on foot was not an overwhelming desire to see their guide's conjectured weeping walls, but Cort's sure knowledge that he would look like a prize idiot for having insisted on coming this far only to turn back at the first indication of difficulty.

To her credit, Shelly was complaining no more than usual. At least they were both somewhat acclimated from the couple of weeks they had already spent in the country. But tramping through the jungle, real jungle, was very different from lounging about at places like the Lopé Hotel, with its fine restaurant and swimming pool and air-conditioned suites.

Dreaming of air-conditioning did nothing to improve his mood. Furthermore, Yacouba was not only leading them through raw jungle but uphill as well. Cort's tone was cutting as he addressed the guide.

"Wouldn't an outpost, much less a castle, have some kind of road or at least an old trail leading to it?"

Yacouba looked back at him. Though he was carrying the tent and most of their supplies, their guide was hardly sweating. "It has been a long time since anyone has come this way except local people, Mr. Cort. Local people do not need roads, and the forest long ago swallowed any trail."

"You're sure you know where you're going?"

"I am sure. The location of the weeping walls is as well known to the people here as it is a place to be carefully avoided. It has been well known as such for hundreds of years." A bit stiffly he added, "It is referenced in several books."

We had damn well better find something substantial, Cort growled silently to himself. If not diamondiferous earth, then a couple of hundred-year-old bottles of rum. Otherwise a certain wise-ass guide was going to find himself handed a pocketful of coins instead of a fistful of Euros when they finally returned to Libreville.

Buttressing tree roots seemed to reach out, deliberately trying to trip them up. Once, they had to freeze and wait for a browsing forest elephant to move out of the way. Later the same day they had to sprint across swarms of driver ants too extensive to go around. The presence of the ant swarms was further proof they were walking through primary, unlogged, untouched forest. The trick was to imitate a ballet dancer, employ the longest strides possible, and leave only the tiniest footprint while dashing across the restless, ever-moving surface. Despite their best efforts, every time he and Shelly found themselves successfully on the far side of a swarm, a few of the ferocious ants always managed to grab hold of a boot and scurry upward to bite and sting. A couple of frantic slaps was usually enough to finish off the isolated assailants.

"What happens if you just ignore the ones that get on you? They're so small. Do they just sting you and then drop off?" Shelly asked as they plodded onward. Even while grumbling and soaked in perspiration she still managed to look good, Cort thought admiringly.

Yacouba peered back at her. "You notice how the ants that get on you always climb upward? They are looking for your eyes."

"Oh." She quickly terminated the line of questioning.

As if by way of compensation for the heat of the day, the first night away from the land cruiser and its conveniences proved surprisingly cool, though just as humid as the daytime. Lying on the ground looking up through the tent's netting, Cort found himself contemplating an endless, tree-framed black sky speckled with thousands of stars that barely winked. After several minutes of this he turned to reach for the undulating shape lying on the foam pad beside him.

An annoyed Shelly swatted his groping hand away. "Are you out of your mind? Until I've had at least two showers and a full bath, you keep your hands to yourself."

He persisted. "The sweat doesn't bother me."

"Then you're more of an animal than any we've seen." Disgusted, she turned over on her side and away from him. The fact that her shoulders were now facing him was in no wise discouraging, but her words were. He decided this was not the place to push that particular envelope. With a grunt, he rolled over onto his back. Small fast-moving shapes were scuttling across the ground all around them, but remained outside the walls of the tent. Somewhere nearby, an exhausted Yacouba snuffled quietly in his sleep.

The sultry, oppressive reality of his immediate surroundings, Cort reflected as he lay still, was not nearly as exciting as had been the contemplation of them back home in Boston. Ah well. Another day would see them reach their mysterious destination. They would have a look around, see what they could pick up, and then start back. At least the stinking hike back to where they had left the land cruiser would be mostly downhill. And as luck would have it, it still had not rained on them.

Not only would sight-seeing in a tropical downpour be uncomfortable, in the midst of a thunderstorm it would be difficult indeed to evaluate any legend of weeping walls.

"This is as far as I go, *m'sieur*."

Cort glared at the guide; if Yacouba chose to run off, he and Shelly would have a difficult, dangerous time trying to find their way back. Even if they succeeded, if their guide beat them back to the car and decided to take off with it ...

"No. You're coming with us, Yacouba."

The man's eyes widened. "Mr. Cort, *m'sieur*, I said I would bring you to the place, and I have done that. But I also said I would not go up to it." He nodded skyward, through the trees. "Soon the sun will be down. I have to start making camp."

Cort nodded curtly forward. "Then set it up next to one of your 'weeping' walls. Wouldn't that be a good place to camp? There might even be some overhead shelter."

Unsettlingly, Yacouba took a step backward. Cort did not pursue—not yet. He had been quite an athlete in college and he was not worried about the guide outrunning him, not even in the jungle. Especially not with all the gear that was still strapped to the man's back. Especially not if he had any hope of receiving the second half of his pay.

Nor did Cort raise his voice. He preferred to persuade with words rather than violence. It usually worked. It had worked with the girls in college, it had worked at the Club, it would work here. He'd always risen to a challenge.

"Come on now, Yacouba. Be reasonable. Remember the remainder of your fee. I think Shelly and I have gotten to know you a little bit over the past couple of weeks. Surely you aren't afraid of some old ruins? This weeping phenomenon—if it's real, I bet I can find an explanation for it. Maybe there's a small spring near one wall. Or a pool of frogs who are more active during a full moon. There are plenty of possible explanations that don't rely on primitive fears."

Yacouba was not swayed. "No *m'sieur*, please, Mr. Cort, sir."

Cort's expression hardened. "You don't come with us, you don't get paid. You get nothing more."

Yacouba looked suddenly angry enough to fight, but Cort knew he was cornered. No government agency would take the guide's side in a dispute with a wealthy tourist. And if Cort ended up hurt, or failed to return to Libreville, none of the promised money would be forthcoming anyway. Shelly stood nearby examining a cluster of yellow flowers and ignoring the confrontation. She did not draw the blossoms close to sample their fragrance. Cort had warned her not to touch anything in the jungle—not even pretty flowers.

Yacouba abruptly seemed to cave in on himself. "All right, Mr. Cort.

I will come the rest of the way with you. As you put it, I have no choice. But please promise me that we will not stay long. You will look, you will see that I told the truth of this place, and then we will leave, *oui?*"

"Sure." With a dramatic flourish Cort stepped to one side. "After you, Yacouba—*M'sieur.*"

His expression grim, their guide resumed the trek forward.

He was as true as his word. They did not have much farther to go. One moment they were completely surrounded by high trees and thickets of denser brush, and the next ...

"Well what the Bingham do you think of that?" Cort halted to marvel. Coming up beside him, Shelly futilely dragged a glistening forearm across her perspiring brow and pushed back her safari hat as she joined him in staring.

"This is what we hiked two days through the jungle to see? A bunch of rocks?" She was exceptionally bummed.

"Not just rocks." Cort's eyes traveled slowly over the structure that rose before them. "They're walls. Real walls." He glanced over at the visibly apprehensive Yacouba. "You were telling the truth about that much, at least."

"Yes, walls. The castle walls." Fearless in the face of nocturnal prowling leopards and hordes of driver ants, their guide was now unashamedly on edge. "We can go now, *oui, M'sieur* Cort?"

Cort studied the wall before them. "I don't see any weeping. I guess we just have to wait for tonight's full moon."

It was amusing to see how big the guide's eyes became. "No! We leave now, *M'sieur*. Cort. Please. You have seen. It is enough."

"It is not enough." Cort was adamant. "Besides, as you so correctly pointed out, it'll be dark soon. Might as well make camp right here. And while you're setting up the tents and starting dinner, Shelly and I will have a look around. Or are you afraid the rocks will eat us?"

"No. No, not afraid of that," Yacouba muttered. Without elaboration and with obvious reluctance, he swung the heavy pack off his back.

"Shelly?" Cort eyed his companion. She shrugged.

"Might as well sweat while walking as sweat while standing."

"Not quite the brisk investigative spirit I was hoping for." Cort started forward.

"You want to see spirit?" She cocked a jaundiced eye at him. "Show me a spa and a salon, I'll show you some spirit."

"In Libreville," he told her. "In a few days. Don't I always keep my promises?" She threw him a look but said nothing.

Though the walls confronting them were formidable, the structure did not resemble a castle in the historical European sense. Fashioned of blocks of neatly cut gray stone that had once been covered by white plaster, the inward-sloping ramparts were now carpeted in green moss so dark it was almost black. Opportunistic fungi thrust stark white caps and beige tubes from cracks where the binding mortar had crumbled away. Crusted with old rust, the protruding cylinders of heavy cannon jutted priapically from bastions at each corner of the impressive fortification. Eying them, Cort marveled at the effort and labor that must have been required to haul the massive weapons up a river and then overland to this remote site.

Of the heavy, double wooden gate that had once barred entry into the inner courtyard, only nails and clasps of failing black iron remained, fallen to the ground where they had been enveloped by eager vines and the questing roots of small trees. The wood itself had long since rotted away, consumed by the voracious, ever-opportunistic jungle. Kneeling to examine the ragged tongues of red-crusted metal, Cort lamented that he was not historian enough to date them. He would have to query Yacouba later. To his untrained eye they looked plenty old. Certainly not twentieth century, he assured himself. Heedless of national laws that forbade the taking of antiquities, he thoughtfully pocketed a few of the smaller nails as he scanned the twilight-lit courtyard in front of him. He had not hiked all this way for nails, even if they did qualify as antiques.

Enclosed by forbidding stone walls three stories high, the courtyard boasted several equally overgrown free-standing stone structures. One clearly had contained living quarters while another was just as self-evidently an old stable. They found evidence of a large communal kitchen, storerooms, a meeting hall of some sort, and a church. As Cort and an increasingly disinterested Shelly explored the ruins' interiors, they found remnants of glazed pottery, furniture, and even a few disintegrating, moldy books. The writing in the latter reminded Cort of Dutch, but the pages were so filthy and worm-eaten he could not be sure.

Any potentially valuable artifacts were notable only by their absence. The nearest to anything of worth they uncovered were a scattering of badly corroded silver spoons and knives. As he continued to pull out and ransack drawers in the kitchen, Cort methodically shoved old silverware into a pocket.

"We'll have another look around tomorrow," he told his companion.

"It's getting dark and I don't want to step in a hole or something. This wouldn't be a good place to sprain an ankle." As he started toward the doorway that led out of the kitchen he was careful to step over the labyrinth of roots that coiled their way across the stone floor.

Following close behind, Shelly paused to pick up half a broken plate. It was white with blue designs. "I hope Yacouba has dinner going. I'm starving."

"He'd better," Cort snapped. "I'm not paying him to sit around and pick his toes. I don't like his attitude lately, either." He shoved a chair aside. Largely intact, it might have been worth something if not for the dozens of wormholes that riddled the intricately carved back.

She ran a hand through the blonde hair she'd deliberately had cropped short for the trip. "Are you going to pay him in full now that he's brought us to this place?"

Cort kicked aside a tin ewer. It clanged noisily as it bounced across the floor. "He certainly thinks so. We'll work it out when we get back to the train station at Ivindo. I'm sure we'll come to an arrangement." He smiled. "Not that he has much choice in what I finally do decide to pay him. Or any leverage."

Out in the courtyard, night overtook the forest like a quiet apocalypse. Here at the Equator the sun did not so much set as plummet below the horizon. Same time every day, day in and day out. To someone used to the gradual sunsets of temperate climes the sudden descent into darkness could be disconcerting. Cort had a small flashlight on the chain he kept in one pocket, but he knew they wouldn't need it. Yacouba had been ordered to set up camp just outside the main gate. Cort had no doubt that regardless of his superstitious fears the guide would do as he had been told. The man had too much money at stake to do otherwise.

So Cort didn't insist they keep going when Shelly declared that she wanted to take a quick look inside one of the portals that beckoned from the inner wall of the fortifications. Several such arching openings formed dark ovals within the overgrown stone. Though clearly intended to permit entry, they had low lintels just like the doorways in the courtyard buildings. People today were taller, Cort knew, than those who had gone before. The opening she chose stood out because of the elaborate gate that hung half-open on massive, bent iron hinges. The heavy black grate looked strong enough to stop a charging rhino.

"Go ahead and have a look," he told her, "but don't linger. I don't know what you think you'll find in there that we didn't see inside the main buildings. And watch out for snakes."

She smiled reassuringly at him, alluring in the deepening twilight despite the perspiration that streaked her face. "I won't be long, I promise. But we came all this way. Maybe there are some diamonds. Or some antique jewelry that got left behind. Something like that would almost make it worth coming all this way!" She gestured skyward. "Anyway, the light's fading. I won't go any farther than I can see. And I'll be careful."

While she bent low to pass under the opening's lintel, he occupied himself examining the ground. The courtyard was paved with large blocks of the same finely cut stone as the outer walls and interior buildings. Someone had gone to a great deal of trouble to erect this imposing fortress here in the middle of the equatorial jungle. Europeans, certainly. Yacouba had been right about that much. Cort had seen pictures of the native-built walls at Great Zimbabwe and this looked nothing like it.

The rationale for the fort's construction remained as much a mystery as ever. If its builders had found gold here, or diamonds, the establishment of such a commanding facility would make sense. Or maybe the driving force had been ivory, he told himself. There were still a lot of elephants in this part of central Africa. He could be standing in the middle of an important ivory trading center whose history had been swallowed up by time and the jungle.

Perhaps he ought to have another, more thorough look at the buildings he and Shelly had just walked through. An ivory storeroom might be situated underground, or otherwise carefully hidden. So far their cursory search had revealed very little in the way of artifacts. It was possible that everything of value had been carried off by various regional tribes. But, he reminded himself, Yacouba was insistent that locals didn't come here.

Ivory held up well over time. He and Shelly couldn't carry off a hoard of tusks, of course, but if they discovered anything substantial it might be worthwhile to come back with porters, even though they would have to be paid handsomely to persuade them to make the trek to this "forbidden" place. If its age could be verified, old ivory was something for which he might be able to obtain a legitimate export permit. If that was the case he knew paying off local officials wouldn't be much....

Shelly's horrific high-pitched scream split the thick, inert evening air and he forgot all about any possible profit that might be gained from the teeth of long-dead elephants.

She was still screaming as he raced out of the central building, the piercing quaver testing the upper register of what the human voice was capable of. It had stopped cold by the time he reached the portal she had entered.

A snake, he thought. Sweat made his shirt stick clammily to his back. She had seen a snake. Or, he worried, she'd been bitten by one. Or maybe she had encountered nothing more than a big spider. Except — her screams had not been screams of fright. Those throaty, bladed trills had been full of pain. Something had—hurt her.

By now the corridor inside the wall had filled up with darkness the way a barrel fills with oil. Had she tripped and knocked herself unconscious? A place like this was likely to be peppered with unmarked cavities. Abandoned, unsealed wells, for example. Despite the confidence she had expressed he realized now he should have insisted that she take the little flashlight.

"Shelly! Shelly?" One hand rested on the corner of the dark portal, the stone damp and cold against his palm as he tried to peer inside. The inner depths were impenetrable, black as the inside of a cave. Extracting the small emergency light from his pocket, he squeezed it to life.

The beam the twin LEDs cast was narrow but bright. He could not see very far ahead, but he could see clearly. Certainly clearly enough to avoid something as obvious as an uncovered well. Unexpectedly, the path he was following began to slope downward. The uneven pavement underfoot was slick with moisture.

It was plain what had happened, he told himself. In the gathering darkness she had lost her footing on the slick cobblestones, slipped, and hit her head. That was why she was not answering his calls. It was a hypothesis that explained her present silence—but not the preceding screams. One scream, yes. Multiple screams ...

The corridor widened, turned a sharp corner, and continued to descend. Soon it had widened enough to accommodate two-way traffic. Heavy iron sconces bolted to the walls showed where torches and later oil lamps had once blazed to illuminate the subterranean maze. Like fossilized flames, sooty streaks rose above each one.

Crazy broad, he told himself. Wandering down into a place like this at sunset. What could have driven her to keep going beyond where the fading sunlight reached? Darkness pressed in tight around him while fingers of damp wormed their way beneath his shirt. Without the flashlight it would have been impossible to see anything.

An iron grate in the ceiling allowed the first hint of intensifying moonlight to illuminate a tiny portion of floor. Until that moment he had not realized how far he had descended. The grate was at least thirty feet overhead.

Where was he? Despite the twists and turns he had taken he was certain he was still somewhere within the castle perimeter. Tilting back his head, he found that he could almost see the rising moon. Still gazing upward, he took a step forward, and stumbled on something.

"Dammit!" Lowering the beam of his flashlight revealed the chain he had tripped over. It lay on the floor in a haphazard heap, as if it had been dropped or fallen from a cart. The links were pitted and heavy. In the feeble light from overhead the iron had a peculiar greasy sheen.

As he continued onward he encountered more of the chains. Many were attached to iron rings that were bolted to the walls but a fair number lay scattered across the floor itself.

Shifting the beam from side to side as he slowly made his way forward, he was relieved when the flashlight finally picked out the pale brown of his companion's pants. He barely had time to register the fact that the pockets were too high and were facing the wrong way. He didn't scream, but that was because he inhaled so sharply he temporarily stopped breathing. Just as he stopped moving.

Shelly was hanging from the ceiling, her legs spread wide. Too wide. A worn, rusted, but still unbreakable iron shackle was clamped tightly around each of her bare ankles. As she swung slowly back and forth, blood flowed copiously down her front and back; soaking her shirt, staining her blonde hair dark, completely covering her face with the same sickly slick sheen. Her eyes were wide open and staring. The left one bulged halfway out of its socket from the sheer force of her shrieking.

She had been pulled apart: split like a chicken wing, her pelvis cracked and one leg wrenched almost completely out of its socket. The brief but intense screams he had heard echoed through him, repeating in his head like a bad heavy metal track, refusing to go away. In the heat and humidity and the cloying, cramping darkness, he found himself shivering. Something had, something had ...

He spun in a panicked circle, the beam of his tiny light catching slashing, brief images of walls, chains, ceiling, floor. Within the subterranean chamber nothing moved. Shafting silently down through the iron grate overhead, cold moonlight etched a crisscross pattern on the stone floor. There was no sound save for the steady drip, drip of blood onto the cold rock.

Then he heard it; the slightest of scraping noises. Something moving over the stone. Sliding impatiently across the same pavement on which he stood. A rough, unyielding, inorganic sound. Not footsteps. Not an animal. There was no soft flesh to muffle the edginess.

He brought his light around sharply to seek the source, and saw the chain coming for him.

Advancing like an iron serpent, it was slithering across the floor in his direction of its own apparent volition. No one was pulling on it, no one was pushing it. Neither was it truly sliding, since it could not slide uphill. In place of a snake head there was a circular shackle of heavy, black, cast iron. A single bolt held the hinged halves together. Fixed in the beam of Cort's flashlight it rose, cobra-like, to regard him. Ancient caked blood lined the inside of the shackle. The bolt unscrewed backwards and the two halves of the shackle parted, opening like jaws.

What the fuck is *that*? His eyes widened.

He might have made a sound. In any case there was no one around to take note of it except the unfortunate Shelly, who was beyond hearing. He stumbled backward, staggering uphill. Something struck at his right calf and a sharp pain shot through his lower leg. Twisting wildly, he looked down to see a second chain starting to wrap itself around his upper ankle. Uttering an inarticulate cry, he wrenched free of the encircling metal and turned to run back the way he had come.

All around him now the sloping subterranean passageway was alive with the brassy clink and clank of wakening metal. Chains scraped and rattled, jangled and clattered as one serpentine shackle after another shook itself to horrid, metallic life. Cort ran as he had never run, trying to keep to the middle of the corridor and away from the walls, dodging the mamba-like strikes of chains heavy and light, flailing madly at those that lashed out as they tried to wrap themselves around his legs, his torso, his thrashing arms.

Somehow he made it out without falling, without being dragged down. Though distant and indifferent, the brightening light of the ascending full moon was as welcome a sight to his wild eyes as the flash and flare of the signs in Times Square on a Saturday night. Behind him, the deep damp corridor that pierced the ground like a junkie's fissured syringe was alive with a rising metallic cackle. Looking back as he struggled to catch his breath in the superheated, cloying air, he saw to his horror that the hideously animate metal Shelly and now he had disturbed would not be satisfied with trying to trap him in the stone catacombs below.

It was coming out after him.

Dozens, hundreds of lengths of chain large and small; some with shackles attached, others adorned with draperies of dried blood, came heaving, writhing, and humping like a horde of gray-black worms out of the arched opening. It was as if a truckload of giant leeches had been dumped into the courtyard. With a cry Cort rushed toward the main gate, howling frantically for Yacouba as he ran. What the guide could do he could not imagine, but if nothing else the presence of another potential victim might at least divert some of the attention of the horror that was tracking him. Risking a glance backward he saw that the metal coils still pursued him across the open stone courtyard.

He shouldn't have looked back.

As a result, he did not see the root that tripped him. It was not animate and did not reach up to grab at his feet, but it might as well have. He went down hard just inside the beckoning gateway. Losing the flashlight as he threw out his hands to protect his face, he managed to break his fall as he slammed forward into the corner of wall where a massive gate had once hung. Slumping to the ground, he grimaced as he rolled over onto his back. The liquid that filled his mouth was syrup and salt. Raising his hands he saw where he had scraped them against the eroded rock. Both palms were bloody. His lower lip had caught the edge of the entrance and was bleeding as well.

Horribly, he was not alone in his silent hemorrhaging.

Blinking away blood and sweat as he pushed back against the moss-covered stone and struggled to his feet, he saw that the wall he had slammed into was wet. Reaching out, he ran his fingers down the rock. When he drew them back they were sticky and sopping. Not with water —it had not rained all day, and it had not rained while he had been underground.

His fingers were covered with more blood. Blood that was not his. It was then that he understood. The walls were not weeping.

They were bleeding.

Eyes wide, holding his gore-soaked hand out away from his body as if mere contact with it would irrevocably find him completely coated with the thick, dark, alien fluid, he struggled to his feet. The moon was rising fast; fast enough to enable him to see the courtyard, the central buildings, and the enclosing inner walls without the aid of his dropped flashlight.

Everywhere he could see, the ancient laboriously worked masonry was soaking wet. Every surface leaked dark red fluid. It oozed from crevices between the stones, bubbled lugubriously from pits in the courtyard, flowed in rivulets and pinched waterfalls from the cornices and carvings that decorated the main structures.

Blood soaked the buildings, pooled up in the stable, filled the fissures and clefts in the paving stones. Blood ancient, but not forgotten. It was the thick liquid ghost of all the blood that had been shed in this place down through the centuries. As it spread outward to submerge the court-yard in all its salty crimson wetness, the chains continued to hump and writhe their way toward him through the rising liquid. Some continued to rise up like snakes, but others—others formed different shapes.

Behind him a pair of small shackles near the ground connected by chains to another pair higher up were attached in turn to a much larger shackle in the center where—a head might fit, he realized in horror. That was when understanding struck him through all the blood and noise and terror and night in which he had become engulfed.

Lives and labor and treasure had not been expended to raise this fortress deep in the jungle to protect trade in gold, or in diamonds, or even in ivory. Castles, the European exploiters and their chiefly native allies had euphemistically called such places. Perhaps to mask the real purpose for which they had been constructed. They had been built to protect, yes. As well as to guard and regulate and look after the most valu-able trade commodity of them all.

Slaves.

He could hear the other sounds now. They were soft and subtle and almost imperceptible, but he could hear them. The hopeless whisperings, the agonized moans, the desperate final cries that rose above the clanking and rattling of the pursuing chains. The echoes of the thousands, perhaps tens of thousands, who had been brought this way, manacled together at the feet and at the neck on their long, sad, one-way march to the waiting distant sea. Torn from their villages by war or raiding parties only to be held here until the time came to send them in armed convoy to the coast. There they would be packed aboard ships bound for Brazil, for the islands of the Caribbean, for the south of North America, never to return. Many would never make it. They would perish from disease or malnutrition or overcrowding during the horrific Middle Passage. Many would not even get that far.

Instead, they would die here, crammed together in subterranean pens of stone and iron, asphyxiated by their comrades in the nightmarish heat and the unimaginable stench of the dungeons. No wonder Yacouba had not wanted to come that last half mile. No wonder he had not wanted to walk those final yards. No wonder.

Cort forced himself to turn, to stay upright. Surely Yacouba had not fled at the sound of Shelly's screams. Surely not! Yacouba would still be waiting for him in the camp in the forest. Once Cort was free of the noisome walls and beyond their suffocating stone grasp he would finally heed the wise counsel of his knowing guide. They would not stay anywhere near here, proximate to this hellhole of horror and death, but would use the light of the moon to lead them away. Across the nearest river, however far that might lie, yes. There they could finally rest, safely distant from the flesh-crawling moaning and the unyielding iron and the weeping, bleeding walls. Shelly—poor broken, dead Shelly—in the darkness below she had fallen into a pit and snapped her neck, he would tell the authorities. Yacouba would corroborate the explanation. Yacouba would not question. Yacouba would go along with anything that let them flee this place and collect the rest of his fee.

Cort went down for the second time just as he emerged outside the gaping portal.

The shackle that snapped shut around his right ankle was attached to a chain whose individual hot-forged links were as thick as sausages. Whining like a trapped dog, he wrenched at it frantically until his already bleeding fingers were torn and raw and more than one nail hung loose and bloody. As he dug at the first chain, a second manacle clamped tight around his left wrist and contracted, dragging him backward while practically lifting him off his feet. The back of his head bounced when it hit the unyielding pavement.

Vision blurring, he looked up and managed to half-focus on the yellow circle of the rising moon. Something blotted it out. It was a heavy neck shackle, four inches wide and half an inch thick, solid wrought iron, supported in an upright position by a coil of bloody black chain. Below it, other chains extended off to left and right. The silhouette they formed was nearly recognizable as that of a human body, a representation in hovering, twisting, restraining iron that stood as a symbol for the thousands who had passed this way, long ago.

The chain that was now secured to his right wrist pulled hard. Very hard. Cort screamed as his shoulder was dislocated. Rolling, desperately moaning Yacouba's name, he tried to crawl back toward the beckoning gateway. In contrast to the intrusive slaving castle that was a hulking artificial blot on the landscape, the fetid surrounding jungle now seemed innocent, pristine, pure. It called to him. It smelled of refuge.

Another shackle clamped shut around his left ankle. Chains snapped taut. He felt himself being dragged backward along the ground, across the hard stones, his unwilling passage lubricated by a layer of blood that was not wholly his own. He tried to dig the tips of his raw fingers into the ground but the smooth paving allowed for no such purchase. The gateway receded in his vision, growing smaller and smaller in the moonlight as his sobbing, desperate form was drawn back into the castle.

From high above the moon looked down, its soft light glistening off the dark liquid that now pooled freely in the open courtyard, shining on the back of the single screaming figure that was being pulled inexorably across the stones toward a single dark, arched opening in the inner wall. The moon had been witness to such sights for hundreds of years and knew that no one escaped from such a place. One could only be marched out, single-file, and that sorrowful spectacle had not been played out beneath its glow for a very long time indeed.

The legs of the figure disappeared into that dark, unfeeling maw. Then the torso, then the head. A last hopeless howl accompanied the disappearance of arms and hands and finally fingers. All movement within the ancient castle walls ceased. Except for the weeping. And the bleeding.

As long as the walls stood, it would never stop.

15 FETCHED

A h, the deep *American South. Where time seems to move a bit more slowly. Where folks remember occasions and occurrences and happenings that the rest of the country, for that matter the rest of the world, have long forgotten.*

Strange things lurk in the backlands of that part of the world. Sometimes hidden, other times right in front of us. We just don't recognize them. Powerful, glad-handing men go about their business with little time for strangers. A few deal in peculiar potions and even stranger notions. They close their doors against certain nights and stay home on eldritch days. They play silver-stringed guitars and thump drums layered with unknown skins.

Their women are often overlooked, but only because they tend to be a bit quieter, a tad more demure. But not always.

Of course, I don't see or hear any such things myself. I just pay attention to the idle conversations and the whisperings. Jot them down mentally for reference and possible future use. Then I leave.

Hurriedly.

It's not unusual to see a dog carrying a bone. Aaron had seen it before. It was less common, however, to see a dog carrying a bone that still had meat on it. Especially if the meat was human and still clad in remnants of the original clothing.

Surely this was a combination to put off an ordinary man. More likely it was a combination fit to send anyone running, wide-eyed and heart-pounding, in the other direction. Any other direction. But Aaron Hepworth was not one to be sent stumbling and screaming through the woods in search of help. Tall, strong, young, a recent college quarterback, scion of a Macon banking family, he was used to confronting problems head on and solving them. Or this case, arm on. Because that was the piece of absent human the dog was carrying.

Trailing shreds of disintegrating cotton cloth and flashing a not-inexpensive watch, the arm sat stiff and straight in the jaws of the mangy canine as it trotted deeper into the forest. At a distance it was difficult to tell which was in a more advanced state of decrepitude: dog or arm. Aaron aimed to find out.

He could envision the headlines now, maybe even bold enough to make the Atlanta Constitution.

"Hepworth Boy Uncovers Forgotten Murder Scene! Police Grateful, FBI Amazed!"

That was assuming the dismembered arm had belonged to a murder victim, Aaron reminded himself, and not some poor suicide or hunter like himself who had perished alone in the woods from an overdose of Georgia tonic. In that event his discovery would still give rise to a head-line, but one that would probably be relegated to Section II of the paper. And not the front page of Section II, either. Nothing for it, he told himself, but to find out.

"Hey! Hey, boy! Bring that here!" Setting his rifle aside, he knelt and whistled. "C'mon boy, bring it here, c'mon!"

The dog stopped to look back at him, a quizzical expression on its distant, tree-shadowed face. Part Australian shepherd, some German shepherd, maybe a little kelpie, Aaron figured. He knew his dogs, which made his father proud. This one was in the worst shape of any dog he had ever seen. Definitely in need of a bath and a thorough delousing. But like any good dog he felt this one would clean up good. Have to catch him first, Aaron knew.

The dog stood staring back at him for a long moment. Then it turned and headed off into the pines once again. Picking up his rifle, Aaron rose and followed. Maybe this way was better. With luck, the dog might lead him to the rest of the body. Poor thing was probably hungry and had dug it up. He didn't begrudge the animal its nibble. Judging from the condition of the dismembered arm its owner wouldn't be missing it, and a dog has got to eat.

But not anywhere around here, apparently. Every time Aaron's long legs closed the gap between them the dog would speed up. Whenever the young hunter fell back, the dog would slow and wait for him. Though frustrated by this ongoing sequence, Aaron found himself admiring the animal's pluck. Not only was it resourceful; it was a gamer.

It was getting dark, but that didn't trouble him. He'd spent many a night out in the woods while hunting. Equipped with gun, GPS, and cell phone, he was confident that he could deal with any problem that might arise. Not that he anticipated any arising.

As he jogged along in pursuit it occurred to him that the dog might be a member of a feral pack. The piney woods of the Southeast were home to many such sorry agglutinations of cast-off canines. This one certainly had the appearance of having long since shrugged off the shackles of domesticity. If it was no longer man's best friend, well, that was its choice. Aaron wasn't worried about encountering a pack. Plug one or two of them and the rest would scatter, howling and with their tails between their legs. Dogs could go wild, but they never went stupid.

He glanced at the sky that was visible between the crowns of the surrounding trees. If it grew much darker he was going to have to utilize the flashlight attached to his belt. The tall pines through which he was jogging seemed to snap tight like slats on a window screen to shut out the fading sunlight.

This is crazy, he told himself. You could spend the night out here, but you don't want to. Take a GPS reading, go back to your truck, and notify the police. You'll still get your headline if they find the body.

Just a little longer, he told himself. There was still daylight. No grungy old dog was going to out-jog him.

The house wasn't much to look at. But then neither was the dog that clip-clopped up onto the front porch, bent its head down, and squeezed humerus, radius, ulna and all through the doggie door that had been cleanly inserted into the solid old wood. Aaron slowed, fully expecting a scream or two to issue from the depths of the wooden structure as soon as its inhabitants got the proverbial look at whut the dog dragged in. But there was only silence. That was odd, and for the first time since catching sight of the animal and its find, Aaron found himself a bit unnerved. But only a bit. Maybe no one was home. As he started toward the modest single-story clapboard structure he took note of the satellite dish on the roof and chuckled in quiet wonderment. Whoever they were, the residents were not as isolated as their location would seem to indicate.

Sturdy and well-maintained, the steps leading up to the porch did not creak. This was no tumble-down shack used only for hunting or recreation. The windows were intact and though flaking, the dull green paint showed clear signs of being periodically renewed. Someone lived here. As if his first impressions were not enough to confirm that supposition, the smell of onions and garlic cooking within sealed his appraisal. He knocked.

He was ready to knock a second time when a voice from within responded. "Come on in, visitor!" The voice was female, he decided, if not especially feminine.

Its owner looked old but not elderly; maybe sixty or so, he decided. The onion-and-garlic aroma came from a kitchen that was set back off to the left of the main living area. There were woven rugs on the hardwood floor, pictures of ancestors on the walls, framed prints of animals and landscapes, and not an Elvis-on-velvet in sight. The place was comfortable, though a long way from the nearest road. Doubtless its owner preferred it that way.

Petite of build, bundled-up hair a swirl of brown and gray, eyes dark and lively, the woman wiped both hands on the apron she was wearing before pulling it off and setting it aside. Short as she was, she had to tilt her head back to meet his gaze.

"Well, sonny, what kin ah do fer you?" She nodded toward the Remington 700 he was gripping. "Hopin' to bag you a buck, are you?"

"Hoping." He smiled. "Not having much luck, I'm afraid."

She smiled. "It's only a couple weeks into the season. Got mine on the second day."

His eyes widened slightly. "You hunt?"

Her laugh was open and infectious. "You choose to live away out here in the woods, sometimes it's easier to catch your own food than hightail it all the way into town." She looked back toward the kitchen, then at her visitor again. "Fresh-kill meatloaf. Don't suppose you'd like tah try some? Mebbee stay for supper? Ah was expectin' the President, but he's busy, so there's a place free at the table."

Fresh venison meatloaf. Vidalia onions. That's what he had been smelling. He started to salivate.

She saw he was weakening. "Ah make a *mean* blackberry cobbler, son. Ah promise it won't hurt you, though."

"What?" Then he got it and laughed. "I like my odds fighting off a cobbler." Finding a suitable spot he set his rifle aside, put his cap down nearby, and began slipping out of his hunting vest. "I'll have to call my friends and tell them not to wait up on me. Do you have cell reception out here?"

She let out a snort. "You joshin' me, boy? These days? Can't get away from the damn things. Use it mahself. Old lady like me livin' alone away out here, got to have one." Her deep, dark eyes twinkled. "You nevah know. Ah might git sick one day."

To amuse himself he dropped his voice an octave, employing the tone that had successfully excised more than one cheerleader's undergarments.

"You're not so old."

"Hellfire, sonnykeep talkin' like thet and you can have the whole cobbler! Wait here just a minute." She turned to go into the kitchen.

"Pardon me, Ms. ...?"

"Mishleen. Mishleen Bokor."

"I'm Aaron Hepworth. Ms. Bokor, your dog—I'm assuming it's your dog—I saw him come through the front door just ahead of me. He was, uh— I don't want to upset you, but it looked for sure like he had a long bone in his mouth and—I think it might be human."

Not unexpectedly her eyes widened and she looked appropriately startled. "Oh, you c'mon now, Mr. Aaron. A human arm?" He nodded, careful to maintain a solemn expression so that she would see he was not joking. "Damn thet dog!" Turning, she headed not for the kitchen but for the hallway that led to the rear of the house. He could hear her stomping around in back rooms and shouting.

"Clairvius! Damnit, dog, git yourself in here this minute! *Clairvius!*"

While she hunted for her animal Aaron waited in the living room. An old-fashioned mantel clock struck the hour. Checking it against his watch, he considered calling his hunting buddies to let them know he would be quite late getting back to the lodge they had rented. No hurry, he told himself. The call could wait until after dinner. Besides, even though Frank and Luther had their own phones set on vibrate, if they were tracking or sitting in a blind staring at a ten-pointer they wouldn't appreciate the interruption. Better to wait until the sun was well down and he could be certain they had finished up for the day.

He was admiring a framed reprint of a leafy tropical landscape when the owner returned, muttering to herself. "Can't find the dog. So can't find this arm you're on about." She squinted up at him. "You *sure* it was a human arm, Mr. Aaron?"

He nodded. "Pretty hard to mistake, ma'am. Still had some sleeve to it."

She shook her head. "The things thet old dog drags up. You reckon on callin' the poh-leece?"

"Eventually. Wouldn't you?"

She pursed her lips. "Expect we'd better find thet limb first. I know the local poh-leece, and ah wouldn't drag the sheriff out here without havin' something concrete tah show him." Her smile returned. "Well, if there is an arm it ain't goin' nowhere. We kin look for it proper after we eat."

Aaron had a sudden thought. "It's a bone, or several of them. What if your dog buries it?"

"Not a problem. I know where thet mongrel does his buryin'. If he done thet, it'll be thet much easier for us tah find it." She beckoned. "Come on in."

The meatloaf was fabulous. There were also fried potatoes, fried okra, rolls and jam, and as a topper the much-promoted cobbler. As he washed down the last of the blackberry with strong sweet iced tea he thought of Frank and Luther back at the hunting lodge the three of them had rented for the week, eating tepid TV dinners out of the microwave. They would not appreciate hearing him tell of tonight's meal half as much as he was going to enjoy telling them about it.

"Wonderful food, Ms. Bokor. That venison meatloaf—if you don't mind giving away a bit of the recipe, what kind of spices do you use?"

"Did ah say it was venison?" She smiled. "As tah spices, I reckon you were probably tastin' the coup de poudre. More cobbler?" His hostess held the metal pan out toward him. It was less than half empty.

"No ma'am, no thanks." He patted his stomach. Normally it was athlete-flat, but not at the moment. "I am stuffed. Not only stuffed." He blinked. "I'm downright tired."

"Good food'll do thet to you, Mr. Aaron." She headed toward the refrigerator with the remnant cobbler. "Want to git lookin' after thet dog bounty?"

"What? Oh, the arm." He started to rise, fell back in the kitchen chair, looked surprised, and struggled to his feet. "Actually, if you don't mind, I'd —I think I'd like to rest for a minute."

She looked alarmed. "You feelin' all right, sonny? Nothin' tah do with mah cookin', I hope!"

"No, no. Just overate a little, I think." He looked toward the living room. His eyes were watering and he rubbed at them. "Mind if I sit in there?"

"Find yourself a comfortable chair. You jest ask me, Mr. Aaron, and ah'll make you some nice hot lemon tea."

"I'll be all right." He smiled, winced slightly, and made his way into the living room. The thick-armed, overstuffed chair he had spotted beckoned invitingly. "Maybe If I just sit for a bit and digest, I can make some room for some more of that cobbler of yours."

She nodded approvingly. "You make yourself comfortable, then. Ah'm jest goin' tah clean up a bit."

He slumped down into the welcoming chair while he listened to her banging and washing in the kitchen. He knew the type: tough old Southern gals who'd outlived their husbands, or had their family and relations slip away and grow distant as they aged. Too independent to move into a retirement community and too stubborn to ask for help. Probably this old home sat on family land on an isolated private tract within the national forest, or maybe it was a lease that had been grandfathered in. After he left he wouldn't worry about her. Any woman who could butcher her own deer could look after herself.

He was wondering who her people were when the dog came ambling in from the hallway with the arm dragging from its mouth. Blood that had not completely dried glistened in the overhead light and tendons hung loose like broken rubber bands. This close, he could see that the fingers were dark, nearly black, suggesting that despite the presence of blood the corpse to which they belonged was old indeed. The contradiction confused him.

Time enough to resolve it later. He started to call out to his hostess, to tell her they would not have to hunt in the dark for the severed limb. He would phrase his words carefully so as to minimize the shock to the older woman.

Then the arm's owner appeared, and the shock he had to concern himself with was not hers.

The man came shambling out of the hallway. With each step it seemed as if he would lose his balance, or stumble into a wall, or trip over cord or carpet. In spite of his side-to-side sway he remained upright. His high-cheekboned face was chiseled and dark, his eyes half-lidded, his thick-lipped mouth slightly parted. For a dead man he was downright hand-some. The sound that emerged from between his lips came from deep within his chest, as if he were a sufferer in the last stages of antibiotic-resistant tuberculosis. At a good six foot seven he was even taller than Aaron, and despite the advanced necrosis that had ravaged his body, still in decent shape. His clothing hung in rags that revealed the shrunken remnants of decaying muscle.

Most conspicuously, he was missing his right arm.

Bending, the giant took a swipe at the dog with his remaining hand. Keeping the scavenged limb clamped tight in his jaws the dog skittered out of the way, growling defensively. It was, a stunned Aaron noted, no more a normal growl than the man's utterance had been comprised of recognizable words. As the lumbering amputee swerved, he finally took note of Aaron's presence. Their eyes locked.

The newcomer's eyeballs were as white and pupilless as piano keys.

Star quarterback, rich man's son, eager hunter; none of that mattered now. Caught in that vacant, blank stare, Aaron screamed. Or tried to. Though he was able to open his mouth, nothing came out. Well, not quite nothing. There was a faint gurgle. Something had flushed his speech and it was going, going, gone down a metaphorical throaty drain.

Hearing the commotion the elderly homeowner emerged from the kitchen. Her gaze took in her seated and unmoving wide-eyed guest, the shambling giant in the center of the living room, and her growling, mangy scavenger of a mutt. She was appalled.

"*Clairvius!*" She started toward the dog, which began backing away. Moving with surprising speed, she blocked the front doggie door, bent, and extended a hand. "Clairvius, give it here! Give it here now!"

Trapped between his owner and the lumbering monstrosity that had emerged from the hall, the dog was still reluctant to surrender its prize. As he made a break for the kitchen the giant lurched toward him, and fell. Snapping sounds ensued as he landed on the fleeing animal. It squealed once and was silent.

Oh lord, Aaron thought, forgetting for a moment his own loss of speech. That thing has killed the poor woman's dog! And what was it going to do to *her*?

The giant's indifference was profound. Rolling off the flattened body of the animal, he sat up, pulled the disarticulated arm from the dog's limp jaws, and commenced trying to cram his missing limb back into its vacant black and red socket. Ignoring these efforts, Ms. Bokor stepped away from the door to kneel beside the body of her dog.

"God damnit, Lucius! Look whut you've done to Clairvius!" She lifted the dog's head off the floor. "You know how long it's gonna take me tah git him up and running again?"

Astoundingly, broken limbs began to twitch beneath her fingers. The shattered tail started to wag, albeit unevenly. And the head—the head that had nearly been separated from the body by the crushing weight of the man who had fallen on it—the head turned and happened to glance in Aaron's direction.

The eyes were as white as Mishleen Bokor's refrigerator.

He tried to scream again, and again failed to utter more than a stran-gled sound. Across the room his rifle stood where he had leaned it care-fully upright in a corner. His thoughts now centered on nothing else, he started for it. Answers he would get, even answers to the impossible, but not until he held the sturdy weapon firmly in his grasp. His hands were resting on the rolled arms of the old chair and he pushed off.

He didn't move.

Propelled by fear, another choking gasp worked its way up his throat to flee his mouth. Try as he would, he couldn't move. He couldn't speak and he couldn't move. The rifle remained where it was, out of reach. The cell phone weighed heavy in his pocket, useless. He fought with every ounce of his being to move something. A finger, a foot, anything. Beyond the ability to blink, open his mouth, and turn his head slightly, he was helpless.

Having left her busted but somehow still kicking dog, Mishleen Bokor was coming toward him. Approaching until she was standing right at his feet, she leaned forward and studied his face. The fingers of one neatly manicured small hand reached for his right eye and he managed to shiver ever so slightly as he tried, tried so hard to get away. Fingertips pushed one eyelid up and the other down as she studied the blue orb. Satisfied, she released the lids and stepped back. A small smile creased her unadorned, slightly wrinkled lips.

"Huh. Poor Mr. Aaron. Musta bin somethin' you et."

Turning, she yelled sharply at the giant. "Lucius! Quit foolin' with your damn arm and git over heah!" She indicated the crushed dog, whose flat-tened body parts continued to writhe and twist as it struggled to stand. Though surely it must have been in terrible pain it made not a sound.

"Clairvius ain't gonna be goin' nowhere on nothin' until I kin git him put back together."

Rising to his full height the giant steadied himself, then staggered over to where the paralyzed Aaron sat helplessly. Slipping his one powerful remaining arm around the motionless guest's back, the big man heaved. Aaron felt himself all but boosted out of the chair. Though his legs would not work he did not fall. Gripping the collar of the young hunter's shirt with one hand Lucius held him upright and without apparent effort.

Walking around in front of them, Bokor studied Aaron's face. His expression frozen in a rictus of terror, he was unable to do anything but stare back at her. A hand reached up to caress him and he could do nothing to forestall it.

"Mr. Aaron. Pretty, pretty Mr. Aaron. It's been awhile since ah've had a young man come a-courtin'. Ah sure am glad you liked mah cookin'. Ah'm afraid the taste'll have tah last you awhile yet." Stepping back, she nodded at the giant. "Put him in mah room, Lucius."

Aaron tried to scream again. It struck him that he had now been bereft of the power of speech for an unreasonable length of time. How long the paralysis that had gripped him would last he had no way of knowing.

The giant hauled him through back hallways into a room that was decorated with an odd mix of the ancient and the new. An iPod player with speakers sat on a dresser beside an old kerosene lantern. Pictures on the walls were more intimate representations of the relatives he had admired in the living room. One weathered black and white photo in a silver frame appeared to show the now terrifying Ms. Bokor clad in the costume of an earlier century, complete to long black skirt and long-sleeved, high necked, pearl-buttoned frilly blouse. But if the era of the photo was accurate, he thought wildly as he lay helpless and unmoving on the bed were the giant had dumped him, then she ought to be not sixty but twice sixty. At least.

How long he lay atop the quilt-covered feather mattress he did not know. He could feel the life not ebbing out of him so much as retreating, shrinking down into a dark hidden place where it would continue to burn, but fitfully. Reduced in intensity, and locked there forever. He had been poisoned, he was certain now, yet he was not dead. He could think but not move. Time, like the rest of his body, had been frozen.

He was certain it was still night when he heard the door open again.

He could not raise his head to look, but he could turn it slightly, and a figure soon came into his range of vision.

Mishleen Bokor had let her hair down. Strange how he had not noticed before that it was long enough to fall to her knees. She was clad in a pale white negligee of fine Belgian lace that did nothing to conceal her sixty-year-old, or twice sixty-year-old, figure.

Bending over him, she began to stroke his brow. He discovered that, somewhat to his surprise, he could still cry.

"There now, whut's all this, Mr. Aaron? Tears? For me? Or for you? You know, usually ah have tah go lookin' fer a date. And here you come, all by your lonesome, without me even havin' to ask. Poor lonely me, who hasn't had a new man in some time now. You'll stay, won't you? Just like you stayed fer dinner? Jest like Lucius and the other young men who came and who stay to keep an old lady company? Ah'll show you some things. We have lots of time. Your friends won't miss you for a while yet. Eventually they won't miss you a'tall. Ah'll take good care of your things. Clairvius is good at burying things where no one kin find them." Her hand moved down from his brow, down.

"You'll have to do whut ah say now, Mr. Aaron. Jest like Lucius and the others. It's better thet way. They like a strong woman who's not afraid tah tell them whut tah do."

He heard the door open again. Expending what little remained of his strength and will, he managed to lift his head slightly so that he could see past her.

The giant Lucius was coming into the room. His expression was as vacant as before, his eyes an everlasting soulless white. Nor was he alone. Those who followed were different yet like him. Strong, once young and athletic, and as empty of eye and incentive as he now was.

Slowly they formed a silent semicircle around the bed, staring, waiting. There were more than a dozen of them, though after the first several an increasingly deranged Aaron stopped counting, stopped looking. The eyes were bad enough. The bodies stank of decay and death, of graves used for sleeping and not moldering. Of diseases that wasted but could not kill, because no virus or bacteria could kill the already deceased.

Mishleen Bokor sounded apologetic. "Mah other gentlemen friends and your predecessors, Mr. Aaron. *Mah* bucks. Ah can't bring mahself to discard them, and after they've enjoyed mah cookin', well, they jest don't fade away. They sort of, you know—*linger.*"

He could not feel her weight as she lay down atop him and began to move, but he could see. His mouth opened wide and he screamed and screamed silently until he could almost but not quite feel the straining in his jaw muscles.

"Ah hope it don't bother you too much, Mr. Aaron, but the undead don't have much tah do, you see, and they like tah watch...."

PREVIOUS PUBLICATION INFORMATION

ABOUT THE AUTHOR

Alan Dean Foster is the author of 125 books, hundreds of pieces of short fiction, essays, columns, reviews, the occasional op-ed for the NY Times, and the story for the first Star Trek movie. Having visited more than 100 countries, he is still bemused by the human condition. He lives with his wife JoAnn and numerous dogs, cats, coyotes, hawks, and a resident family of bobcats in Prescott, Arizona.

IF YOU LIKED A TASTE OF DIFFERENT DEMENSIONS

Oshenerth

The Flavor of Other Dimensions

The Gamearth Trilogy
by Kevin J. Anderson

OTHER WORDFIRE PRESS TITLES BY ALAN DEAN FOSTER

Oshenerth

The Flavor of Other Dimensions

Our list of other WordFire Press authors and titles is always growing. To find out more and to see our selection of titles, visit us at:

wordfirepress.com

CPSIA information can be obtained
at www.ICGtesting.com
Printed in the USA
LVHW092323080519
617201LV00001B/19/P

9 781614 759850